Royal

Soulless Kings MC
Book 10

Andi Rhodes

Blue Journey Publishing

Copyright © 2023 by Andi Rhodes

All rights reserved.

No part of this book may be reproduced in any form or by any electronic or mechanical means, including information storage and retrieval systems, without written permission from the author, except for the use of brief quotations in a book review.

Cover Artwork - © Amanda Walker PA & Design Services

Edited by Darcie Fisher.

This is for anyone who has learned the hard way to never judge a book by its cover. Clichés are clichés for a reason.

Okay, okay... maybe judge an actual book by its cover 😜

But remember, I've already licked them all!

Also by Andi Rhodes

Broken Rebel Brotherhood

Broken Souls

Broken Innocence

Broken Boundaries

Broken Rebel Brotherhood: Complete Series Box set

Broken Rebel Brotherhood: Next Generation

Broken Hearts

Broken Wings

Broken Mind

Bastards and Badges

Stark Revenge

Slade's Fall

Jett's Guard

Soulless Kings MC

Fender

Joker

Piston

Greaser

Riker

Trainwreck

Squirrel

Gibson

Flash

Royal

Satan's Legacy MC

Snow's Angel

Toga's Demons

Magic's Torment

Duck's Salvation

Dip's Flame

Devil's Handmaidens MC

Harlow's Gamble

Peppermint's Twist

Mama's Rules

Valhalla Rising MC

Viking

Mayhem Makers

Forever Savage

Saints Purgatory MC

Unholy Soul

A note from the author:

How is it possible that we're at book ten in the Soulless Kings MC series? It seems like only last week that the idea was born, yet here I sit, typing this note and getting ready to hit 'publish' in order to wrap up the series. I had no clue how deep into the world of SKMC I would go or how much a part of me the SKMC family would become when Nicole Cypher and I started Fender (book #1), but my gut told me it would be an amazing ride. And it has been.

I have y'all to thank for that. Because of your absolute love (or obsession lol) with the SKMC, I was able to continue a series that I love, that I am obsessed with. But all good things must come to an end.

The very first words that came to my mind when starting to write this series were *'They say your life flashes before your eyes at the moment just before death. They fucking lied.'* Seventeen words dragged me out of my comfort zone and so profoundly changed who I am as a writer. And those seventeen words ushered in an era that is now drawing to a close.

Royal wasn't always a planned part of this journey. Hell, a lot of the Soulless Kings' brothers weren't. Despite that, he quickly wormed his rich, horny little heart into my head and refused to be silenced. But his story isn't like the others. It's not paved in bad childhoods or trauma. Royal doesn't have a sad and depressing backstory. He's simply a piece of the Soulless Kings puzzle that needs to be put into place in order to be complete.

I didn't plan for no trauma or simple. I never plan for that. I planned gut-wrenching and twisty. But Royal and Paige pretty much told me to fuck off. This book is unlike any other in that I restarted it several times because the characters demanded it of me. They made it very clear that I needed to write *their* story, not the one I thought should be their story.

And their story is what you're about to read. It's an enemies to lovers tale of two souls who did not meet under the best circumstances, and I hope you love it!

So, without further ado… grab a glass of wine (or a vodka cranberry) and enjoy the ride!

Much love,

Andi

Prologue

It was the night that everything, and nothing at all, changed.

Paige
Seventeen years old...

"You look great."

I roll my eyes at my best friend. She's not even looking at me because she's so focused on her reflection in the mirror. She looks incredible, as always. The tight silver dress is cut low in the front revealing her cleavage, and the thin straps show off the smattering of freckles spread across her shoulders. She's perfect, and I'm... not.

Alice and I met in kindergarten, and we've been inseparable ever since. Well, almost. When Paul, the captain of the football team, asked her to be his girlfriend earlier in the school year, I started playing second fiddle in her life. But not tonight, at least for this little snippet in time because she's here, at my house, getting ready for prom with me.

I lift my cell off my mattress and check the time. Paul

and Jordan, my date for the dance, will be here any minute. I step up next to her so I can look myself over one more time. My simple black dress doesn't hold a candle to hers, but it's all I could afford. Unlike her, I don't have parents who throw money at me in an effort to make me disappear so they can entertain their important friends.

Alice is the rich one, the pretty one, the one who always gets what she wants. And I'm just me, Paige Watkins, captain of absolutely nothing. I don't attract attention, don't have money, or insanely good looks. I'm average, nothing special.

"Are you going to the after party?" Alice asks me absently.

"You know I'm not. I have to work in the morning."

"Girl, you make little brats smile for the camera," she scoffs. "Not exactly rocket science."

Alice doesn't have to work so she's never understood why working at Castor Photography Studios is so important to me. That's okay because she doesn't have to understand. I love working there. Not only am I learning so much from my boss to prepare me for becoming a photographer, but I genuinely enjoy every aspect of the work. It doesn't feel like a job.

"Maybe not," I concede. "But it pays for my cell phone and car insurance. That's not nothing."

"Whatever."

"So, uh, is Paul going to the party?" I ask. I don't give a crap, but I'll talk about anything if it changes the topic and gets the focus off me.

Alice laughs, and the tinkling sound fills my room. "Of course he is." She grins. "And guess what?"

"What?"

Alice leans in close and whispers, "Tonight's the night."

"The night?"

"*The* night, the one where I... *you* know, do *it* for the first time."

"I thought you and Paul already... you know."

Alice shrugs. "I've sucked his dick, but that's it. He keeps pushing for more, and I'm gonna give it to him."

I chuckle. "Well, just don't be stupid."

"OMG, Paige. You sound like you're thirty, not seventeen. You need to live a little, my friend." She rests a hand on my shoulder. "And I know just the thing."

I eye her suspiciously. "What?"

"Jordan, duh. I mean, he's not Paul, but he's not terrible." She turns to face the mirror again and applies more lipstick to her already bright red lips. "You should totally come to the party with Jordan and bang him. At least you wouldn't have to say you're a virgin anymore."

"But you're a virgin," I remind her.

Alice bounces her eyebrows. "Not for long."

"Paige! Some boys are here for you and Al."

"I really wish your mom would stop calling me Al." She shudders as if horrified. "It's annoying."

"You try telling her that. She doesn't listen to me."

"Whatever." Alice picks up the small clutch she brought and walks to the door. "Let's go impress our guys."

Twenty minutes later, I'm sitting in the back of Paul's dad's Mustang with Jordan. Alice is in the front with Paul, and she can't keep her hands off him. If I'm not mistaken, she's giving him a hand job, if the way her arm is moving is any indication.

Several seconds later, Paul grunts, but then pulls her hand out of his pants and shoves her arm away. If that's how she gets treated after doing something like that for him, I want no part of it.

"So, Paige," Jordan begins, pulling my attention to him. "You coming to the party tonight?"

Why is this party so important to everyone? It's not like there won't be others.

I shake my head. "Can't. I have to—"

"She's coming," Alice says as she turns in her seat. "At least for an hour or two."

"That's great," Jordan says.

"Yeah, great," I mumble.

"In fact, before you guys picked us up, she was telling me how excited she is to spend more time with you."

I'm gonna kill her. I am. I'm going to yank down one of the pointed stars I know will be hanging from the gym ceiling and shove it into her throat.

"Really?" Jordan's face lights up. "I bet you'll get some really neat pictures there. You did bring your camera, right?"

"You know I did. You watched me put it in my purse before we left the house," I remind him.

For someone so smart, he's very stupid.

"Cool."

No one speaks for the rest of the drive, and the only sound is the music Paul cranks up and my thundering heartbeat. When we arrive at the high school, the parking lot is already full. Paul slings his arm around Alice, and Jordan holds my hand while we walk inside.

The dance itself flies by, and everyone seems to have a good time. Paul is crowned King, and that upsets Alice because he has to dance with the Queen, which is not her. To be fair, Paul is a senior and Alice isn't. Only seniors are allowed to be crowned.

She gets over it though when Paul whispers something in her ear afterward. She giggles at whatever it is, and all is forgotten. Paul could cheat on her with the entire cheerleading squad, and she'd forgive and forget. That's how stupidly in love with him she is.

"You ready to go?"

I turn toward Jordan, who hasn't left my side all night. I can't help but be skeptical of his reasoning. Like I said, I'm not the girl who attracts attention. So why do I have all of his?

"Oh, um, yeah." I set my half-empty cup of punch on the closest table. "How are we getting to this party?"

"Same way we got here."

"Okay."

I guess I'll have to call my mom to pick me up later because there's no way I'm staying all night. I can't.

"Paul will let me use the Mustang to take you home," Jordan says, as if he read my mind. When I stare at him, he shrugs. "You said you have to work tomorrow, so I figured you'd want to go home tonight."

I smile. "Thanks."

Jordan lifts my hand. "No problem."

The ride to the motel where the party is taking place is quick, and my nerves kick into overdrive when Paul pulls into the parking lot. My palms are sweaty, and my entire body feels stiff.

You're going to a party, not a public hanging.

I wish I could tell you that I held onto that thought, but when Jordan pops my cherry a little over an hour later, I can't help but wonder if a hanging would've been more fun. Unfortunately, Alice and Paul both got so drunk that Alice went home still a virgin, so there was no reason for me to feel the pressure I did to have sex.

Maybe there is a silver lining in all of this though. For once, I did something before Alice. And it involved a guy.

That alone is worth the very uncomfortable two minutes with Jordan.

Prom night is supposed to be the best night of a teenager's life. It wasn't mine, and as I got older, I realized I wasn't alone in that. But it *was* the night that set the tone for the next ten years of my friendship with Alice.

It was the night that everything, *and* nothing at all, changed.

Chapter One

I'll be fucking damned if my mistakes put the club in jeopardy... again.

Royal

Ten years later...

"How do you want to handle this?"

I press my arm harder into the throat of the shitstain I've got held against the brick wall and glance at Piston. As the highest-ranking Soulless Kings member in this alley, it's his call how this plays out, so I'm not sure why he's deferring to me.

"C'mon, Royal," he cajoles. "You're the prospect recruiter. Make a fucking decision."

I look beyond Piston, toward the main road, and then dart my eyes in the other direction, concern with being caught riding me hard. We don't typically handle club business out in the open like this, but when problems arise, they need to be dealt with as quickly as possible. And Tom is a problem.

A walking, talking, breathing *problem.*

I level my gaze on Tom. "Who was that you were talking to back there?"

Piston, Squirrel, Gibson, and I stopped at the bar on our way home from a long day of riding. We hadn't gone anywhere in particular, just down the coast since this morning dawned warm and sunny for the first time in almost a month. Most of the brothers opted to ride north with their ol' ladies, but Holland, Sylvia, and Alena were too busy with other things to take the day and go. Gibson suggested stopping off for a drink before heading back to the clubhouse, but before we could even enter the bar, trouble made itself known.

"I wa-wasn't talking to an-anyone," he stammers, his eyes wide, and his breath reeking like he's been on a week-long bender.

Lifting my knee, I nail him in the nuts, and he gags when he instinctively leans forward and is caught up on my arm.

"Lying isn't gonna help you," I snarl. "Let's try this again. Who the fuck were you talking to out in front of the bar?"

"Dude, you've gotta see how bad this is for you," Squirrel comments. "Tell him what he wants to know."

"I wasn't tal—"

Gibson's fist flies past me and connects with Tom's nose. "Try again," he barks.

Blood pours from the man's nostrils, and he sputters when it reaches his mouth. When it drips from his chin and onto my shirt sleeve, I grin.

"Tom, Tom, Tom," I sing-song. "Clearly you don't have a problem talking, so why are you holding back now?"

Tom turns his head to the side and spits out some blood.

Royal

When he faces me again, his eyes tell me all I need to know... he's ready to talk.

"He was a nobody," he says with resignation. "Just some random drunk who was camped out in the doorway next to the bar."

"Jesus," Piston mutters and turns to Gibson. "Go see if you can find the guy."

Gibson and Squirrel take off down the alley, and I glare at Tom. "You've caused all sorts of trouble."

"I don't want any trouble."

Ignoring him, I glance at Piston. "We don't have a choice, do we?"

My VP shakes his head. "Nope. Not anymore."

Taking a deep breath, I tip my head back and stare at the sky. This was such a good day, and now I'm in a fucking alley that smells like piss and bad decisions, about to murder someone. Don't get me wrong, it's not the killing I've got a problem with. Being a patched member of a one-percenter motorcycle club has given me a front-row seat to all sorts of violent acts. But the location is never this... public.

I roll my neck to look at Piston again. "Got your knife on you?"

"Knife?" Tom asks, fear overwhelming in his tone. "Wh-why do you need a knife?"

Piston bends and when he straightens, he holds out the serrated blade I watched him tuck into his boot before we rode out this morning. "Will this do?"

"I'd prefer my gun." I shrug. "But that'll be quieter. I don't trust that the music blaring from the bar will cover up the shot."

I stretch out my free hand and take the weapon from him before pressing the tip into Tom's stomach.

"You don't have to do this," Tom cries, his words annoyingly clear for the first time since we grabbed him fifteen minutes ago. "The guy is a drunk. He won't remember what I told him. And I won't talk to anyone else. I promise I won't. My lips are—"

"We got a live one!"

Both Piston and I whip our heads toward the alley entrance. Squirrel and Gibson are laughing as they haul a man toward us. The man is struggling to get free of them, but it's no use. He's no match for the two of them. Hell, I doubt he'd be a match for a five-year-old with how stumbling drunk he is.

"Keep your fucking voice down," Piston barks.

"Run!" Tom shouts. "Get away fro—"

I shove the knife into his gut and savor the way he grits his teeth against the pain. When I twist the blade, his bugged-out eyes remind me of a cartoon. He tries to open his mouth and speak, but I lift up on the knife and grin like a fool when his breath stutters to nothing.

After yanking the blade from him, he slumps to the ground in a heap. Ignoring the corpse, I turn to Gibson and Squirrel. Before the man being dragged through the trash-filled alley can protest what he has to know is coming, Gibson wraps his hand around his throat and chokes him to death.

When the drunk is as dead as Tom, Gibson lifts his stare to Piston, who's staring at him with a shocked expression.

"What?" Gibson asks.

Piston shakes his head with a laugh, but it's Squirrel who responds.

"Bro, didn't know you had it in you."

Gibson shrugs. "Figured we've made enough noise."

"This is not at all how I figured this day would end," I say matter-of-factly. "Want me to call Parker for clean-up?"

"Ya think?" Piston chuckles. "I should make you clean it up. Tom became a problem because you thought he was a good recruit."

"I can handle it."

"I know you can, Royal. That's why you're wearing a patch." He slaps me on the back and then grabs his knife from my hand. After he bends to wipe the blade off on Tom's jeans, he shoves it back into his boot. "Call Parker and get him here. Tell him to bring Benny," he adds, referring to one of our newer prospects. "You can head home once they get here."

"Don't worry, man," Gibson adds. "Someday you won't be low man on the totem pole."

I chuckle. "I know. It's why I'm recruiting as hard as I am."

Not long after receiving my patch, Fender and Piston called me into the office like a damn kid getting called to the principal's office. I entered that room terrified that I'd done something wrong, but when I came out, I was higher than a fucking kite.

There'd been talk for a while that we needed to beef up our numbers, but it's always fallen on every brother to make that happen. And then they all started dropping like flies into the marriage pool, leaving them less and less time to focus on finding fresh blood.

Apparently, after I was patched in, the others had voted in favor of assigning one brother to the job of recruitment. With no ol' lady, or even a girlfriend, I've got all the time in the world. Which means I was unanimously voted as the lucky bastard to hold the title of Prospect Recruiter.

I fucked up with Tom, but I recruited Benny before him, and he's working out great. So as I lean against the wall and wait for him and Parker to arrive, I remind myself not to get too worked up over the dead fucker at my feet.

Mistakes happen. I'm human, and I'll make more of them. Countless more, no doubt.

But I'll be fucking damned if my mistakes put the club in jeopardy... again.

Chapter Two

Hindsight is twenty/twenty.

Paige

"Do you need me to do anything else before I head home for the night?"

I smile at Evelyn, my assistant. She's the best hiring decision I made when I took over Castor Photography Studios. If it weren't for her, I wouldn't have been able to take the studio as far as I have.

"Nah, I'm good. Go home and get some rest. We've got a big day tomorrow."

"Okay. If you're sure." She starts to pack up her bag, and I shake my head. I swear she takes more work home than anyone I know, despite me telling her it isn't necessary. "I'll be here by seven tomorrow morning. The Harris-Neal wedding is our biggest event to date, and I want to make sure everything goes off without a hitch."

I stifle a giggle. "Pun intended?"

"Intended? No. But it was good, wasn't it?"

I laugh at her, and she joins in. "Everything is gonna be great. You've worked hard to help me get ready. Just enjoy your evening."

"And what are you gonna do to relax?"

I think about the voicemail on my cell from Alice and know what I'm *not* going to do.

I shrug. "Probably open a bottle of wine and a good book and take a bubble bath. Same thing I usually do the night before a wedding shoot."

Bubble baths, books, and bubbly is my pre-wedding routine. It helps to put me in the right frame of mind to capture the most important and romantic day of my clients' lives. And let's face it... I don't have a ton of personal experience to fall back on in the romance department.

"Just promise me you won't go out with Alice."

Evelyn hates Alice. Not that Alice has ever done anything to my assistant to warrant that hatred, but Evelyn is nothing if not loyal to me. And spending time with Alice seems to put me in a sour mood lately. At twenty-seven, she still acts like she's nineteen with no responsibilities.

"Promise."

"Good." Evelyn grabs a slip of paper off the counter and hands it to me. "Then I can give you this. It's another message from Alice."

I groan. "How many times did she call today?"

Evelyn darts her eyes away and when she returns them to me, her shoulders sag. "Four. Well, not including the calls you missed on your cell. I quit counting after six of those."

Alice doesn't quit. For as long as I've known her, she's been pushy. I determined years ago that her parents are mostly to blame for that. The only attention she ever got from them was when they would hand her money and send her on her way. Once I realized that, I vowed to be the one person who is there for her, no matter what.

And it's exhausting.

"Thanks, Ev." I finish packing up my cameras for tomorrow as I speak. "I'll talk to her again about not calling the studio."

"Good luck with that," she snips. "Alice is like a dog with a bone." She slings her bag over her shoulder. "Anyway, have a good night. I'll see you in the morning."

Ten minutes later, I'm turning off the last of the lights and locking up the studio for the night. As I walk to my car, I pull up Alice's most recent voicemail, the only one I didn't get a chance to listen to yet and try not to let my frustration get the best of me as she talks.

"Paige, c'mon, answer your damn phone." Alice sighs dramatically. "Brock and I are going to that bar downtown that I love." Brock is her boyfriend of three years, and as much as Evelyn hates Alice, I hate him. He's an asshole who always seems to find trouble. "I know you've got that wedding tomorrow, so you don't even have to stay out late. Just one drink. I promise."

It's never just one drink.

Alice drones on for another solid minute and when the voicemail ends, I delete it like I did the others.

The drive to my loft passes in a blur as I recall one of the last good moments in my friendship with Alice.

"You're not seriously considering this, are you?"

I stare at Alice and can't help but wonder if she knows me at all. I've worked at Castor Photography Studios since high school. Why is it so hard for her to understand my desire to make the business mine now that Stuart is retiring?

"Of course I am," I say, and as hard as I try to sound

confident, I know considering it is all it is. "But I doubt it'll happen."

"Is it really what you want, though? To be responsible for an entire business? If it fails, that's on you."

"If it fails?" I repeat incredulously. "You don't think I can do it?"

"No, of course not," she insists. "I know you can. It's just..."

"What, Alice? It's just what?"

Alice sighs but straightens her shoulders. "We're still young. You've got the rest of your life to work yourself into the ground."

"Maybe. But how often does an opportunity like this come along?"

I might only be twenty-three, but I'm not the social butterfly she is. Photography is my passion. Always has been. My place in the world is behind a camera.

"If it's what you want, I support you." She reaches out and squeezes my hand. "I'll always support you."

I force a smile. "I know you do. And I appreciate it. It doesn't matter though," I say with a dismissive wave of my hand. "There's no way I can make an offer that won't be insulting to Stuart."

"Why not?"

I huff out a breath. "Seriously? I'm not exactly rolling in money. Shit, I'm barely flush. And I don't have credit, so a loan is out of the question."

Alice's eyes light up. "Maybe I can help."

My heart pounds in my chest at the possibility, but I quickly dismiss it. "Yeah, right. You think this is a horrible idea, Al. Why on Earth would you help me with something you don't even agree with?"

Royal

"It's not about me agreeing with it, Paige," she insists. "You're my best friend, so I want to help."

I eye her suspiciously, wanting to hope that this is the lifeline I need to take my career to the next level, but also wondering if she's just messing with me. She says she's my best friend, and she is, but she's also self-centered and spoiled, and spending her money on anything that doesn't directly benefit her is out of character.

"How would this work exactly?" I ask, giving in to the possibilities.

After pulling into the underground parking garage beneath the building where my loft is, I shift out of drive and lean my head back against the seat.

How would this work exactly?

I'd give anything to have not asked that question. Hindsight is twenty/twenty though, and I couldn't have known at the time how fucked of a situation I was putting myself in.

Taking a deep breath, I pull on the handle and get out of the car to head inside. I toss my purse on the kitchen island and focus on getting something to eat. The bottle of white wine in my refrigerator taunts me as I reach for the leftover grilled chicken I made for dinner last night. Wine is my typical go-to, but for some reason, it doesn't appeal to me at all right now.

While my chicken heats in the microwave, I grab the vodka I keep on the top shelf of a cupboard. I pour a healthy amount into a highball glass and add in some cranberry juice. Once I've got food and drink, I walk into the living room and collapse onto the couch.

It doesn't take me long to fill my stomach and by the time I'm ready to draw a bubble bath, I'm also a little tipsy. Vodka cranberry hits me much faster than wine.

After drawing a bath, I strip out of my jeans and panties

and kick them into the corner of the bathroom. I take off my flannel shirt and yank my tank over my head, tossing them into the ever-growing pile of laundry.

Climbing into the tub, I submerge myself into the warm water and let the heat soak through to my muscles, inch by inch. My head swims from the minimal alcohol, so rather than read like I usually would, I simply enjoy the silence until the water cools and my skin turns into something resembling a raisin.

Ten minutes later, I'm curled up in bed with my comforter pulled up to my chin. It crosses my mind to send Alice a text and at least acknowledge the fact that she called, but I quickly dismiss it. Texting will lead to a phone call, which will lead to me feeling guilty for ignoring her all day, which will lead to absolutely zero sleep.

You have nothing to feel guilty about.

Oh, how I wish that were true.

* * *

"Thank you so much for making this day extra special."

I accept the hug from the new Mrs. Neal, doing my best not to brush up against her cheek and ruin her makeup. All of the wedding party photos have been taken, but there's very little time before the reception starts, and absolutely zero time for touch-ups.

"You're very welcome," I tell her with a smile. "But you've got a lot of day left."

She beams up at her husband, who is so smitten with her I might as well not even be in the room. Which is exactly as it should be.

"We're all loaded up."

Turning to the doorway, I see Evelyn leaning against

the frame, a no-nonsense look on her face. George, the second photographer I hired to help out with all of Castor Photography Studios events, stands behind her. He's got a camera strap looped around his neck, and he looks at Evelyn and me like a father would a daughter. He's always happy and supportive, which makes him perfect for occasions like weddings and parties.

"Thanks, Ev," I say before turning back to look at Mr. and Mrs. Neal. "George is going to stick around and snap any candid shots he can as you two prepare to head to the reception. Evelyn and I will meet you there."

The rest of the day goes smoothly, and as the newlyweds are hustled into their car at the end of the night, I can't help but be proud of how absolutely perfect everything turned out. I take the last photo of the event, a beautiful shot of the couple as each of them leans out through the windows on either side of the limo and waves to their friends and family.

I envy the bliss on their faces, the happiness that seems to drip from their smiles and float through the air back toward the crowd. I want what they have, what all the couples I photograph have. But my focus is on my business, and that makes me happy in a completely different way.

Evelyn and George help get all of our equipment packed into the bags and then Evelyn's car. She'll bring everything to the studio on Monday, and that's when I'll start going through every single shot, one by one, and pick the most special for my clients.

By the time I turn onto the street my loft is on, I'm beyond exhausted and ready for bed. I go through the motions of parking the car, walking across the road to my building, and stepping onto the elevator. When I reach the level my loft is on, I've got my key out and ready, but I pull up short when I see the light filtering under the gap between the large metal sliding door and the floor.

I definitely didn't leave a light on.

I check, and the door is still locked, leaving only one explanation: Alice.

Taking a deep breath, I shove the key in the lock and go inside, only to be greeted by my pacing best friend and her boyfriend. As soon as Alice spots me, she rushes to my side. Her face is pale and void of any makeup, so I know something is very wrong.

Brock, on the other hand, looks cool as a cucumber.

"They're dead, P," Alice cries, latching onto my arm and practically dragging me to the couch. "Those guys in the alley... two of them... they're dead. Stabbed, strangled... Oh my God."

"Alice, what are you talking about?" I ask. "Who is dead? What alley?"

"Calm the hell down, Alice," Brock snaps as he steps up next to the couch. "This isn't all that bad."

I narrow my eyes at him while Alice pulls herself together. If I weren't so tired, I might make note of the fact that she's able to do so rather quickly, but I'm too focused on Brock and his cavalier attitude.

"What isn't all that bad, Brock?" I demand. "Who is dead?"

Alice lifts my hand and squeezes it. "We need your help, P."

"Would one of you please tell me what the fuck is going on? First, you're rambling about dead people and now, you want my help. I'm lost."

"Right." Alice sighs. "Let me back up. Last night we went to that bar downtown for a few drinks. We ended up hating the place, so we went back to the one beneath my apartment for an hour or two before calling it a night."

"Okay," I say, drawing the word out.

"Anyway, it was warmer last night, and my AC is out, so I had to open the window."

"Damn," I mutter. "It must have been stifling in your apartment for you to do that. You hate the smell that comes from the dumpsters in the—" I press my lips together as something clicks. "The alley," I finish.

"Exactly," Brock says. "We were about to fuck when a noise caught our attention."

I cringe at his crassness, but I'm not surprised by it. Alice might not have had sex on prom night, but she's more than made up for it since then. And Brock likes to flaunt their escapades.

"And that's when they killed him, P," Alice adds. "Just stabbed him in the stomach and let him die."

"Who?"

"I don't know who he was," she admits. "I recognized the guy they strangled though. A drunk who spent more time on the streets than he did with the wife who used to come pick him up at the bar."

I glare at Brock. "How isn't this 'all that bad'?"

"Because we saw who did it," he says casually, like that explains everything.

Darting my eyes back and forth between the two of them, I try to make sense of what I'm hearing. "You went to the police, right? They've been arrested?"

"Well, not exactly," Alice says quietly. When I glare at her, she softens her expression. "We called the police, but by the time they got there, they'd already moved the bodies."

"Who is 'they'?"

"The Soulless Kings MC."

My stomach does a somersault before dropping to the floor. This is a nightmare. Everyone in Oregon knows who the Soulless Kings are, what they're capable of. And it's common knowledge that they can do whatever they want and get away with it.

I've seen a few of them out and about, and I don't personally have a problem with them, but I'm also a stranger to them. A non-issue. If I don't piss them off, they have no reason to do me any harm.

"You know as well as we do that they've got certain cops in their pockets," Brock says. "There's no way they don't find out that we called in the murders. No fucking way."

"They're gonna come after us, Paige," Alice says, the stark fear from when I first saw her returning to her eyes.

This can't be happening.

"But we have a plan."

I lift my eyes to Brock. "A plan? You have a—"

"We blackmail them," he spits out. "If we blackmail them, they go away. And we come out ahead because not only are we safe, but we get rich."

I press my fingers to my temples to stave off the headache throbbing just beneath my skin. I wish I could shut out the world, shut off my blind loyalty to Alice so this would all go away, but I don't know how. And because of that, I'm in this whether I like it or not.

All the things I said about Alice are true. She's spoiled, self-centered, and...

She made your dreams come true.

What I wouldn't give to have never taken that money from her. It doesn't seem to matter that I paid her back within the first year because the studio is very successful. It doesn't seem to matter that she doesn't rub it in my face that she did that for me.

What *does* fucking matter, even if it shouldn't, is that I can't seem to ignore the fact that I love her like a sister. I'm the one person who's always been in her corner, although she didn't always deserve it. I don't want to help them with whatever scheme they've cooked up, but I know as sure as I know humans need air to breathe, I'm going to help.

Because she gave me my dream. She made it happen. Without her, I have no clue where I'd be now. Certainly not in a cushy loft with a thriving business that I love beyond measure.

I'll help them because I have to.

I take a deep breath and force a smile at Alice.

"What do you need me to do?"

Chapter Three

I'm a horny asshole, what can I say?

Royal

Two weeks later...

"This turned into a hell of a party."

I tip the beer bottle to my lips and down what's left before slamming it on the bar top. One of the things I took to the brothers after being named Prospect Recruiter was the idea of open house parties, where we open our doors to whoever wants to come hang out. I wasn't exactly expecting any of them to be on board with it, but they all voted in favor of the parties and now the events are a monthly occurrence until we get our numbers where we want them to be.

"It did," I agree, grinning at Piston.

He glances around the main room of the clubhouse as he finishes off his beer. "I've gotta admit, I was skeptical when you suggested this whole open party bullshit. But it worked out. Benny is great, and I think Dillon is fitting in."

Royal

Benny was recruited from the very first party, and he's quickly proving himself. And I recruited Dillon at the last event, having realized within the first thirty minutes he was here that he would make a damn good Soulless King. It's easier for me to see potential in people that others might not because I was that hopeful not that long ago.

"Did he tell you that story about his principal yet?" I ask, laughing at the memory of Dillon animatedly relating the details to several of us earlier in the week.

"Which one?" Piston asks with a chuckle. "The time he broke into the prick's house or the day he and some of his friends tacked condoms all over his office walls?"

"That was fucking hilarious," Flash says as he steps up next to Piston. "Who the fuck stakes out their principal's house based on a rumor that the douche is a wife beater?"

"A future Soulless King, that's who," Squirrel, our tech guru, says as he enters the conversation. "Good thing he did too from the sound of it. When he heard shouting through the windows one night, Dillon broke in to save the wife from flying fists."

Piston shakes his head. "Then he dragged the man out to his little beater truck and threw him in the bed. Drove him straight to the police station and then testified against him when the guy went to trial."

Fender and Charlie join our growing group. "Are you talking about Dillon?" our Prez asks.

"Yep."

"I fucking love his style," Fender adds with a smirk. "I just wish there were pictures of all those condoms." He slaps me on the back. "You did good, Money Bags."

I groan at the nickname. The Soulless Kings are fully aware of my wealth, and they tease me about it relentlessly. But for whatever reason, it hasn't tainted their view of me.

Sure, when I first started prospecting, it seemed to be an issue, but now that I'm a patched member, no one bats an eye at the wad of bills I always have on me.

Yet Fender continues to use that stupid nickname.

"Royal, Prez," I remind him, although there's no heat in my tone.

"Man, I know that. I gave you the damn road name," Fender snaps with a smirk. "But Money Bags gets your panties in a wad."

With a roll of my eyes, I turn and lift my hand to Parker. "Another beer, Prospect," I call out to be heard over the music.

"Coming right up," he shouts.

As my brothers stand around and talk about Dillon and Benny, I watch the room. It's a packed house tonight, and several potential candidates have already made the rounds. I've got my eye on two guys who rode in on Harleys, decked out in biker gear. At first, I thought they were wannabes who were trying way too hard, but after talking with them earlier, it's clear they are bikers to the core.

But are they Soulless Kings?

That's the million-dollar question. Breaking from the others, I make my way through the crowd toward Sully and Bruno. I need to focus on them tonight, see how much I can learn so when we vote on them at our next church session, I've got enough information for the club to decide.

Before I reach them, the unmistakable rumble of a motorcycle cuts through the music, pulling my attention toward the door, which is propped open so we can see who's coming and going despite everyone checking in with Pony at the guard shack.

The single light of the bike is bright, but the two headlights from the vehicle following it are slightly dimmer. I stride to the entrance to watch as they park on opposite ends of the lot, and Fender joins me.

"Fucking hell, that bike sounds sexy," he comments before tipping his beer to his lips.

Charlie, his ol' lady, seems to appear out of nowhere and grabs both our arms to drag us outside.

"C'mon, boys," she says with excitement. "You've gotta check out this Harley."

"Wait, you know who that is?" I ask, nodding toward the man straightening next to the motorcycle.

"Is this the guy?" Fender asks.

Charlie groans as she continues to lead us toward the man. "You guys are idiots. Do you really think I'd get this excited about someone I don't know?" When she halts next to the bike, I'm finally able to get a good look at the dude and his ride. "Guys, this is Brock," she says. "Brock, this is Fender, my husband and club president, and Royal, the prospect recruiter."

Fender whistles as he walks a circle around the Harley. It's tricked-out and painted a glossy black, with an almost pearlescent orange swirl, and has shiny chrome accents. It's a nice bike for sure.

"You did this?" I ask Charlie.

She works at Infinite Motors, the club-owned custom bike shop, and she's turned into one of the best we have for custom paint jobs.

"She sure did," Fender says proudly. I chuckle at how his chest seems to puff out like a damn peacock.

"Maybe I should let you have a go with Tyche," I tell her, referring to my own Harley. I named her after the Greek goddess of fortune and luck, and let me tell ya, she has delivered. "I've been wanting something a little different."

"Bring it in whenever," Charlie says with a wink. "You know I prioritize brothers' bikes. I'll have Tyche turning heads in no time."

"It's definitely the best money I've ever spent," Brock says, reminding me that he's there. I sort of forgot with all the fuss over his motorcycle. "And I was happy with how fast the turnaround time was."

Fender shakes his head. "I knew it would be good when she spent more nights at the shop than in our fucking bed."

"How did you not see this?" I ask Fender. He works at Infinite Motors too. Hell, he and Charlie co-own it, and he's there almost every day.

"Char wouldn't let me near it."

"Only because I had a very specific vision, and I knew you'd put in your two cents." She leans into Fender and wraps her arm around his waist. "I was gonna show you, but Brock picked it up before I had the chance. So I invited him to come to tonight's open house party to show it off."

"I appreciate the invite," Brock says with a grin. "It's not often I get to hang out with people who understand my love of riding."

"You're gonna be surrounded by gearheads tonight, that's for sure," I tell him.

"Sounds like a great party."

I whirl around toward the sultry voice and immediately swallow my tongue.

Holy fucking shit.

Standing before me are two women with their arms linked. The taller chick is the most scantily clad woman I've ever seen. And that's saying something because the Bangin' Betties are rarely in anything more than barely there scraps of cloth.

"Eyes are up here," she says, but her voice is slightly higher pitched than the one who spoke earlier.

I lift my head and grin, unashamed to have been caught ogling her tits. Her lips are painted a bright red, and her smile is almost blinding. And all I find I want to do is stare at the areolas peeking out the top of her black lacy tank.

I'm a horny asshole, what can I say?

"I hope it's okay that I brought them with me," Brock says from behind us.

She leans forward, so close I can smell the hint of strawberry in her shampoo, and stretches her hand out. "I'm Alice," she says, and I shake her hand.

I glance at her friend, who's staring at me with eyes that scream 'not gonna happen'. "And you are?"

"I'm Paige." And there's that voice, the one that had my dick twitching in my pants.

"Royal," I manage and then glance over my shoulder. "It's an open house, so it's fine that you brought them."

"But we wouldn't have been allowed to come otherwise?" Paige asks, her tone suggesting annoyance.

Okay, a sexy voice does not equal pleasant.

I take a moment to admire her natural, girl-next-door looks. She's wearing ripped jeans, a black and orange flannel with a tank underneath, and black boots. Her dark blonde hair is pulled into a wayward ponytail, and from what I can in the minimal lighting, she doesn't wear much makeup.

She's a stark contrast to Alice. While Paige's voice makes me lose the ability to think, it's Alice's looks that keep my attention. They're both sexy as hell, but only one of them gives off 'not spending the night alone' vibes.

Alice slaps Paige on the arm playfully. "Be nice," she

says with a giggle and then lifts her eyes to mine. "Sorry. She's not usually like this."

"Good to know."

We all make our way across the lot toward the door. Charlie is engrossed in conversation with Brock about his Harley while Alice and Paige blindly follow them. Before I can step inside, Fender grabs my arm to stop me.

"I do *not* envy you, Money Bags," Fender says with a laugh.

"Why's that?"

"Because the second you heard Paige speak, you got pussy-stupid." He shakes his head. "And then there's Alice. Not who you really want, but the easier conquest for sure."

"That about sums it up."

"There'll come a day when women like Alice just won't cut it. And today ain't that day, is it?"

"Nope."

"Just make sure she's not taken first," he warns me. "I didn't get the impression that Brock is dating either of them, but ya never know." He shrugs. "Maybe he's not like us and all over his woman when she's around."

"Not a problem, Prez," I assure him. "I have no interest in sloppy seconds."

When we step inside, I search the crowd for the three newcomers. They're dancing in the center of the room, but Alice seems more interested in Paige than Brock. And Brock seems more interested in his surroundings than either chick.

He's either the most hand-off boyfriend I've ever seen, or Fender is right and he's not dating Alice or Paige.

I weave my way toward them, one thought on my mind.

Time to find out who's sleeping in my bed tonight.

Chapter Four

Blackmail. Just get the damn blackmail.

Paige

"He's coming this way."

I move to the beat of the music, doing my best to ignore the pounding of my heart against my ribs. When Brock and Alice told me they had a way to get the blackmail they need to keep them safe, I had no clue what to expect. I'd hoped that nothing would ever come of their whole plan, but I should've known better when Brock went out and bought a used Harley just so he had an excuse to go to Infinite Motors.

"Try not to be such a bitch," Brock says, a weird glint of warning in his eyes. "He seemed to like you."

I shiver at the thought. I wish I could say it's because the thought of a murderer liking me is revolting, but that's only part of it. Royal isn't at all what I imagined when Alice described the scene in the alley to me.

He's panty melting hot.

"He was staring at your girlfriend's tits," I remind Brock coldly. "I can't believe you let him do that."

"It's fine," Alice assures me. "Just... take out your phone and start taking pictures. There are so many people here, no one will think twice about it."

Taking a deep breath, I reach into my pocket and wrap my fingers around my cell. Before I can pull it out, Royal appears next to me.

"So," he says as his eyes dart between me and Alice. "Which one of you is dating Brock?"

Alice shifts her gaze to her boyfriend, who's out of Royal's line of sight, and Brock subtly shakes his head.

"Neither of us," she replies coyly and steps closer to the biker.

"Is that right?" Royal snakes an arm around her waist and pulls her close.

Stunned by his boldness, I watch as the two of them sway to the music. Alice turns and presses her ass against his groin, and I can't stop my gaze from lowering to see if he's affected by her.

Yep. Boner alert.

Brock clears his throat before grabbing my arm. "Why don't we go get a drink, Paige?"

It's on the tip of my tongue to refuse, but his glare stops me. I don't know how either one of them are okay with this, but the longer I'm here, the clearer it becomes that they will do anything to get what they want.

And they want to keep their lives. Is that so bad?

"Sure. I could use one," I finally say. I turn toward my best friend and shout to be heard over the music. "Don't do anything I wouldn't do, Al."

"Oh, sugar, she will," Royal says, lust in his tone. "If I have anything to say about it, she definitely will."

"I'm fine," Alice says with exasperation. She spares me a glance and smiles. "I promise."

"C'mon, Paige."

Brock tugs on my arm so I force my feet to move. I am not comfortable with any of this, but I remind myself that there are both club members and outsiders present, so nothing bad will happen tonight. Well, nothing other than my very not single friend screwing a murderer.

At least she'll still be breathing.

When we get within a few feet of the bar, Brock stops and turns around to watch Alice. His eyes narrow on them, and it's the first hint he's given that he doesn't like her flirting with another man.

"Go get me a beer."

Brock's order grates on my nerves, but I grind my teeth and bite my tongue. Getting into an argument with him is not the way to go about not drawing attention to myself. I already screwed the plan up with my attitude outside. Alice isn't who was supposed to garner Royal's favor.

I guess I should've listened when she tried to get me to wear one of her outfits. Maybe then he'd be nibbling my neck instead of hers.

Stop it!

"Paige," Brock barks.

I shake away my wayward thoughts and face him. "Yeah?"

"Beer."

I turn on my heel to step up to the bar. All the preparation I did for tonight, the shows I watched, and books I read... none of it comes close to the reality of being at a party at an MC clubhouse.

Because TV and books are fiction, idiot.

I thought for sure fear would dominate my senses, but I don't feel afraid. Which is insane considering why I'm even here in the first place.

After waiting for several minutes, the bartender makes his way over to me.

"What can I get ya?" he asks with a friendly smile.

"Just a beer, please."

"One beer, comi—"

"She'll also have a..." The man sitting on the stool to my left looks me up and down as if to assess my alcohol tastes and then looks at the bartender. "I don't know, Parker. Whaddya think?

Parker takes his turn eyeing me up and down, making me feel very exposed. "Vodka cranberry, right?"

I swallow my shock. "I... How'd you guess?"

Stool Man laughs as he slaps his palm down onto the bar. "My man here is a cop. He knows all."

"*Was* a cop, Greaser," Parker bites out. "*Was* a damn cop." He returns his attention to me. "But he's right. I was an undercover cop in a previous life. I learned how to read people real fucking fast."

Seriously? Does he know about the murder?

"Go get her that drink and the beer," Greaser orders, and Parker walks away to do just that.

"Just the beer," I call out to him, but he ignores me and starts pouring the liquor into a clear glass.

"Don't listen to her," Greaser shouts louder.

Staring at him, I paste a smile on my face. "Thanks for the drink, but I'm good."

"I've been watching you since you walked in, and you look like you need some liquid calm." When I open my mouth to protest, he holds a hand up. "No strings attached.

I've got an ol' lady who would put my balls in a vice if I flirted."

"Yet you admit to watching me for the last what, thirty minutes or so?" I arch a brow.

"I like to know what's going on around me," he says unapologetically.

"So why the drink?" I ask, genuinely curious.

"Because Trinity would squeeze that vice a lot fucking tighter if she knew I sat back and watched a woman get treated like a damn lackey." Greaser cups his junk and shudders. "Especially in a place where women are treated and protected like the queens they are."

"I see." I look over my shoulder at Brock but refocus on Greaser when I see that I'm not being observed. "Well, thank you. But like I said, I'm good."

"Here ya go," Parker says as he sets both drinks in front of me before moving away to talk with a few of the other bikers.

"So, he your boyfriend or something?" Greaser tips his head at Brock.

"What? Me and Brock?" I shake my head vigorously. "No. God no. He's Alice's..." Fucking hell, I need to shut up. "He's a friend of Alice's. We're all friends."

You're going straight to Hell for all these lies, Paige... among other things.

Greaser eyes me suspiciously but doesn't question my words. I take a sip of the vodka cranberry he ordered me and pray the liquor stops my palms from sweating and my nervous thoughts to stop clanging around in my brain.

"Paige, what's the holdup?"

I take a step toward Brock, but Greaser puts his arm out to stop me even as he stands from his stool. He steps between us and folds his arm over his chest.

"Mind if I give you some advice?"

Brock shrugs. "Go for it."

"Get your own fucking drink next time."

"Excuse me?"

Greaser fists a hand in the front of Brock's shirt and pulls him close. "I'm guessing you're here because you wanna be one of us. Well, if that's ever gonna happen, if you wanna be welcomed into the fold as a brother, then get your head outta your ass and treat people, women in particular, with respect."

Brock's shoulders stiffen. "Respect? You're all a bunch of crimi—"

"I suggest you don't finish that sentence," Greaser barks. "What we do, what we stand for, is not your business unless we make it your business. And that's still up for debate." He shoves Brock away from him. "We might be one-percenters but that does not make us bad men."

Greaser is called away by another man before Brock can respond. Which is probably a good thing considering the murderous glare Brock is sporting.

"Hypocritical prick," he mumbles before drinking down half his beer.

Takes one to know one.

"What did you say to him?" he asks me, turning his anger on me.

"Nothing."

He stares at me a moment longer and then shakes his head. "Whatever. Just go get us that blackmail so we can get the hell outta here."

Brock grabs the beer from my hand and returns to staring at Alice.

Don't, Paige. Don't argue. Just get some pictures and then this can all be over. Alice's life depends on it.

Royal

I repeat that in my head over and over again as I down the rest of my vodka cranberry and set the empty glass on the bar. Pulling my cell out of my pocket, I walk across the room toward the far wall. And when I face the crowd again, I begin snapping pictures of everything and everyone.

Blackmail. Just get the damn blackmail.

Chapter Five

Good fucking luck.

Royal

"I really am sorry about my friend earlier."

I glance over my shoulder at the bar. Paige is currently talking to Greaser, and jealousy weighs on me. Shaking off the feeling, I shift my gaze to Brock, who is laser-focused on us. I pull Alice closer, and lean next to her ear.

"You sure Brock isn't your boyfriend?" I ask before easing away to look at her face.

Alice grins. "Would I be flirting with you if he were?"

"Then why is he looking at you like he wants to lay you out on the bar and eat you for a midnight snack?"

She waves her hand dismissively. "That's just the way he looks." She presses her lips together for a moment before sighing. "Okay, if you want to know the truth, he wa—"

"I insist on the truth, Alice," I tell her. "People who lie to me tend to hate the consequences."

Her throat muscles work as she swallows, and her eyes darken with... fear? She recovers so quickly that I'm able to convince myself that I'm imagining things.

"Noted." She presses closer to my chest. "Now I don't know whether to keep being honest or to make some shit up. Consequences can be fun," she purrs.

"The kind I dole out aren't," I deadpan.

Alice's gaze darts from me to Brock and back again, and I swear her skin pales as she clears her throat. "Lucky for me, I've been nothing but honest." She dips her head, overplaying the coy act. "Brock isn't my boyfriend." She lifts her head and locks eyes with me. "Anymore."

Something about her tone raises the hair on the back of my neck, but my dick screams at my brain to stand down. I haven't been laid in weeks and apparently, he's starting to get impatient.

There's not always danger.

I choose to believe her. It's dumb, and I'll probably end up with an STD for my stupidity, but that's what Gibson is for, right?

"So the rage that's rolling off of him in waves is justified?"

Alice shakes her head. "No. It's been several years since we were together like that. He's just protective of me."

"What is he protecting you from?"

She drags her fingertip from my chest to the top of my jeans. "You."

"If he's so protective, why'd he bring you?"

Alice stops moving and pouts. "Do you really want to spend the night talking about Brock?"

Yes.

No.

Fuck.

"Not at all."

She lifts her hands to my shoulders and rises on her tiptoes to press her lips to my chin. "Good." Alice shifts her mouth to my ear. "Maybe someone should be protecting you from me."

"Maybe so."

I slide my hands up the back of her tank but freeze when a flash of light catches my attention. Lifting my head and scanning the room, I see that Paige has moved and is currently snapping pictures of the party.

"Oh, hell no," I mutter as I move Alice to the side.

I stride toward Paige, fury pumping through my veins. These types of parties may be new, but there's no way Pony forgot to tell someone about the no picture rule. He's too paranoid to forget something that important.

Paige gasps when I yank her phone from her hand.

"What the hell?" she cries and goes to grab the device. "Gimme that back!"

I hold the cell out of her reach, which isn't hard because she barely reaches my chin. "Who gave you permission to take pictures?" I demand as I scroll through the last few photos she snapped to check for anything that shouldn't be caught on camera.

"I don't need your permiss—"

"That's where you're wrong, sugar," I snap, ignoring the anger-fueled terror written in her expression. "Unless approved by Fender, no one is allowed to take pictures inside the clubhouse. And I know he didn't give you the go-ahead."

"I'm a grown-ass woman," she seethes with a stomp of her foot. It's cute, and I try not to chuckle at her. "I'll do whatever the hell I want with my phone."

I glare at her, and she glares right back. Neither of us

waver, and I have to admit, I'm a little shocked by that. She doesn't strike me as a fighter. Smart-mouthed and sassy, yes. But not a fighter.

"Give me my phone," she snarls.

"What the hell is going on?" Alice asks as she steps up next to me. "Paige, what did you do?"

Paige's eyes widen and she stares at her friend. "What did I do?" she asks, her voice not at all calm.

Alice places her hand on my arm and pulls it down so she can take Paige's cell from me. She proceeds to scroll as I did, and then, with a hand on her hip, stares daggers at Paige.

"You heard the guy at the gate, P. Why would you take pictures when you know we aren't supposed to?"

"You've gotta be—" Paige presses her lips into a thin line and turns her head to avert her eyes. After several deep breaths, she faces us again, and there are unshed tears in her eyes. "Ya know what, forget it." She yanks her phone out of her friend's hand and proceeds to delete all the pictures she took, making sure I can see the screen as she does. When the screen defaults to the most recent saved photo, I stare at the image for a second, but then her snarky voice pulls me out of my stupor. "Better?" she snaps.

I stare at her, wondering why she's so upset, and absently nod. "Yeah." Shifting so I can see the rest of the room, I realize we're being stared at. Swallowing past the uncomfortable desire to go back several minutes and handle this whole situation differently, I scrub my hands over my face. "But I still have to ask you to leave."

Why are those words so hard to utter?

"Really?" Alice asks, pushing her tits against my arm. "The pictures were deleted. Just let her stay."

I shake my head. "Rules are rules."

"It's fine," Paige says quietly and focuses on Alice. "You and Brock stay," she insists. "I'll take the car, and you can ride with him."

Before I can stop her, Paige shoves past me and rushes to the door, where she disappears into the night. I take a step to go after her, feeling like a total douchebag because of the tears she refused to cry, but Alice stops me.

"Let her go, Royal," she instructs. "I'll go check on her in a minute."

"But she's leaving. She shouldn't be driving upset."

Why am I arguing about that chick?

Alice sighs. "I'll go."

She turns to go after Paige, but Brock is suddenly there, blocking her path.

"Where are you going?" he demands.

"I'm gonna go check on Paige."

His eyes slide to me, and his jaw tenses. "What the fuck is your problem, man? I could hear you shouting at her from the other side of the room... over the damn shitty music."

My blood boils. I don't know if Charlie truly thought this guy would fit in with the club or if she just wanted to show off her work, but he never should've been invited.

I step up into his space. "You better back the fuck down and remember where you are," I snarl. Brothers begin to circle us, clearly sensing an issue. "Paige broke one of only two rules we have for these parties. No running your mouth about what happens here, and no pictures. She took fucking pictures, and I can't abide that."

"Since when do you give a fuck about Paige?" Greaser asks from his position a few feet away. "You sure didn't seem to give a shit when you ordered her to get you a beer."

Brock stiffens, but he focuses his stare on Alice. "We're leaving. Let's go."

Alice, God bless her slutty soul, straightens her spine, pushing her tits out. "Get a grip, Brock. You're the one who wanted to come to this party in the first place," she says. "I'm not quite ready to leave yet, so if you want to, I suggest you hurry up and take Paige on your bike and leave me the car."

The image of Paige on the back of this asshole's bike is like a match to my already boiling blood. I pull away from Alice and move toward the door.

Turning so I can walk backward, I ask, "You got this, G?"

Greaser nods. "Go make sure she's okay. And for fuck's sake, apologize for ripping into her. She seems like a nice girl."

A nice girl? I don't know that I'd call her that, but she's intriguing. And the photo that was on her screen, the one of a woman in a wedding dress in what looked like a dress shop, has set off all sorts of questions to zig-zag through my mind.

She's not easy. Paige isn't how you get laid tonight.

Fuck getting laid. The only thing on my mind at the moment is making things right so some woman who doesn't give two shits about me at least leaves knowing I'm not a total prick.

Good fucking luck.

Chapter Six

Guess I'm gonna need to figure out how to become a spy in under twenty-four hours.

Paige

You heard the guy at the gate, P. Why would you take pictures when you know we aren't supposed to?

Of course, I heard the fucking guy at the gate!

How could Alice do that to me? How could she throw me under the bus so completely to a man who she should be terrified of?

How could you be attracted to a man you should be terrified of?

The night air is cool against my wet cheeks, so I swipe the tears away. When Royal snatched my phone out of my hand, my brain went on the fritz. I forgot that I was supposed to be afraid of him and barreled head-first into pissed the fuck off.

I'm still pissed off but even more than that, I'm embarrassed. I pride myself on being strong and independent, and

Royal

I've had to be in order to make the photography studio successful. But here I am, crying like a little girl who had her favorite toy taken away.

Leaning against the side of the building, I try to settle my breathing. I close my eyes and imagine I'm in my darkroom at the loft, watching as my latest photos develop into the captured moments they are. I picture the self-conscious grandma who came to me last year because she wanted to give her husband 'something special' for their fiftieth anniversary and was plunging into the world of boudoir. Her smile at the final result fills my subconscious.

Weddings and events may be what pays the bills, but it's those one-off clients, those individuals who want me to capture what amounts to a single second, a single ka-chick of the camera shutter, who drive me forward. What they see as ugly or not worthy of the time it takes to snap a picture, I see as immense beauty.

"I know it's short notice, but I need you to do it anyway."

The feminine voice cuts through the noise in my head, and I force myself to stand stalk still as if that will help me hear better.

"Yeah... right... the old bottle factory just east of the city..."

I hate when people use speakerphones because it's always that one lady who's chattering to her best friend in the stall next to me while I'm trying to poop, but I'd give anything for this chick to use the feature now.

"Of course, he knows I'm asking you," she snaps. "Fender wants backup since it's a new buyer, but he needs people who won't raise suspicion."

Backup? New buyer?

"I won't be back to the clubhouse beforehand, so you'll

have to meet up with us a few miles away from the site. No bikes and no cuts... Yeah... It should be quick... ten-thirty tomorrow night... No, no, just..."

"Paige?"

Startled, my eyes fly open, and I find Royal staring at me with a mixture of curiosity and concern. I push off the wall and stalk to the driver's side of my car, which is only a couple vehicles away.

"Do you always sneak up on women in the dark?" I snap over my shoulder.

"What?"

I yank open the door, but before I can climb in, Royal is spinning me around to face him. My chest heaves with annoyance, and I narrow my eyes at him. All I can think about is the woman on the phone at the side of the building and how much it would suck if she came around the corner now.

Please don't come around the corner. Please don't get m—

"I came out to make sure you were okay," he says as he removes his hand from my arm. The disdain in his gaze from earlier is gone, that look of rage at someone daring to break the rules. Right now he just looks... kind.

And it's unsettling.

"I'm fine."

He shoves his hands in his pockets and rocks back on his heels. "You don't look fine."

"Gee, thanks."

"Are you always this hostile?" When I continue to stare, he continues talking. "Look, I'm sorry. I shouldn't have barked at you like I did about the pictures. It's just..."

"Apology accepted," I force out. "Can I go now?"

I have to go. I have to process what I heard and whether

or not I should see it as a sign to run and run far or to take advantage of the knowledge and get the blackmail for Alice and Brock.

"Do you ever stop?"

"Stop what?"

"Putting up walls, being snarky when someone is trying to be nice." He shrugs. "I don't know. Don't you get tired of being angry?"

I'm not angry. Not usually.

And you're not supposed to be nice. You're supposed to be a criminal.

Your eyes aren't supposed to be friendly. They're supposed to be murderous.

"I'm not doing any of that," I tell him. "I just don't appreciate being yelled at in a party full of people, and I really hate when my best friend doesn't back me up like I do her."

As soon as the words leave my mouth, I want to call them back.

"Sounds like a conversation between you and Alice, not you and me."

And therein lies the problem because I won't have that conversation with her. I've spent years having her back, protecting her from feeling like she has no one, and doing whatever I could to help her.

"Tell me about that picture on your phone," Royal says, seemingly out of nowhere, pulling me from my thoughts.

"I deleted the damn pictures," I remind him, frustrated that he's going back to that.

"Not those pictures." He removes his hand from his pocket and grabs my cell from me. Just like inside, he holds it out of my reach when I try to take it back. After several long seconds of him turning in a circle and me stupidly racing around him, he stops and turns the screen to face me. "This one."

I freeze as the image immediately transports me back in time.

"You look incredible, honey."

Darla, the bride, beams at her mother and best friend. I lift my camera and snap several shots of her face, as well as theirs. Not all brides take advantage of my pre-wedding package, but when they do, I get so excited.

"What do you think, Paige?"

Lowering my camera, I smile. "Nope. I just take the pictures," I say with a chuckle. "I don't offer an opinion."

Darla rolls her eyes. "Oh, c'mon," she pleads. "I really want to know what you think."

"I think..." I glance at her mom and friend, who are both looking at me expectantly. "I think you look stunning. Darren is going to lose his mind when he sees you."

Darla claps her hands together with excitement. "Yay. That's exactly what I want to happen."

"So, is this dress the one?" her mom asks.

"I think so, yeah."

Darla steps off the pedestal that is a fixture in all bridal shops and walks to her mom to give her a hug.

"Go get changed, honey. We have some celebrating to do," her mom says cheerfully when she steps back from the embrace.

Just as Darla pulls the curtain closed to the dressing room, a cell phone rings. I make a habit of leaving mine in my car when I'm with a client, so I know it's not mine. The ringing stops and Darla's voice carries out to the rest of us.

"I can't wait for you to... Yes, this is his fiancée... Who did you say this was?"

Silence ensues for what feels like an eternity. Her mom

and friend have made their way to stand outside the curtain as if sensing something is wrong.

"This is some sort of joke. It has to be. Darren can't be... Yes, I understand. Okay."

Another few seconds pass before the curtain is slowly opened, and Darla steps out. Her face is pale, and her eyes are brimming with tears.

"Darla, honey, what's wrong?"

"She was so fucking happy that day," I say, lifting my gaze to Royal.

"Was?"

"Not five minutes after I took that picture, Darla got a phone call from the hospital in another state where her future husband had traveled to for work." I sniff back tears as I recall the anguished scream that tore from her when her mother asked her what was wrong. "He was rushing to the airport so he didn't miss his flight home and got into a car accident. He died in surgery to repair his injuries."

Royal's shoulders seem to deflate. "Damn. That's awful."

I nod absently. "It was."

"Why do you keep the picture on your phone then?"

"Because it reminds me that beauty is everywhere." I grab my cell when he hands it back to me and stare at the smile on Darla's face. "I know this particular photo doesn't show the ugly side of beauty, the pain that comes when the good things are ripped away from us, but I know it happened. People see this picture and all they see is a happy bride-to-be. I look at this picture and see all the tragedy that came after. And yet... it's still beautiful."

"That's deep."

I huff out a laugh. "Yeah, it is. And it's true." Remembering that I'm supposed to be scared and mad, I toss my cell onto the car seat and square my shoulders. "Can I go now?"

Why the hell would you tell him all that? He's not who you bond with over deep thoughts or the meaning of life.

"You are an enigma, Paige."

"And *you* are a dick," I say matter-of-factly.

"I can't exac—"

"Paige!"

Turning toward the entrance to the clubhouse, I see Alice rushing toward me as Brock walks in the opposite direction toward his motorcycle, and I stiffen. Royal glances over his shoulder, but quickly looks back at me.

"You're not happy to see her," he observes.

Warmth spreads through me at his words and for a moment, I want to warn him. I want to tell him to watch his back with Alice and Brock. He's judgmental and infuriating, but I don't know why he did what he did. Maybe his victim tried to hurt him first.

"You should know, Alice and Br—"

"We need to go," Alice says when she reaches us and threads her arm through mine. "Coming here was a bad idea."

No fucking shit.

"I'm ready when you are," I tell her, my warning for Royal forgotten. It's not like I can spill the beans with Alice right here.

Royal's eyes dip to the swell of Alice's tits, and whatever weird moment passed between us over that picture dissipates and my goodwill toward him because of his damn kind eyes and observant nature evaporate. I chalk it all up to idle chit-chat and remind myself that he zeroed in on Alice from word one.

I've got my camera and apparently, Royal has his dick.

Royal

Without another word, Alice and I get in the car and when I shut the door, Royal steps back. He watches as the engine roars to life, and I see him in the rearview mirror, still watching, as I drive down the long road to get the hell out of this place.

"Did you get any more pictures?" Alice asks ten minutes later.

"What?"

"Pictures, Paige," she says with exasperation. "You were outside for a few minutes before that asshole chased after you. I hope you took more pictures for blackmail."

Rather than answer with the words that are on the tip of my tongue, I think of the phone call I overheard. There's some sort of meeting tomorrow night at the bottle factory. I know exactly where that is, and it's definitely not the site where anything good takes place.

"You do know that's why I pretended to be mad at you, right?" Alice asks, concern lacing her tone.

"Huh?"

"I wasn't really mad back there, about the pictures," she explains. "But I remembered what that guard guy said about being kicked out if we broke any of the rules, so I figured it couldn't hurt to try and get you some alone time with your phone."

That's why she did that? She was acting?

With a sigh, I nod. "Of course, I knew what you were doing," I lie.

"Are you sure? Because last time I checked, you can't cry on command, and there were definitely tears in your eyes."

I laugh off her concern. Really, what else can I do? Admit that I thought she betrayed me? I don't think so.

"I'm sure, Al. It's all good."

Alice smiles and leans back in her seat. "Good. Because Brock is pissed, and I can only take one person I love being mad at me at a time."

Her words hammer home why I stick by her, no matter the consequences to myself. Reaching across the seat, I grab her hand and give it a squeeze.

"We're good. Promise." I pause for a moment while I navigate getting on the interstate, but then continue. "But I didn't get any more pictures. I was going to, and then Royal was just there, so I couldn't."

Alice sighs as she shrugs. "It's okay. We'll figure something else out."

"Did Brock get an invite to prospect for the club?" I ask, shamelessly hoping that he did so I don't have to do something I might not come back from. "That would make it so much easier."

"Hardly. Royal definitely doesn't like him. And neither do some of the others. Even that Charlie bitch who invited him to the party in the first place got in his face there at the end."

Not surprising.

I squeeze her hand again for reassurance.

"I'll figure something out, Al. Okay?"

"I know you will. You always do."

Guess I'm gonna need to figure out how to become a spy in under twenty-four hours.

Chapter Seven

Free, shallow, easy.

Royal

"We were gonna scope the place out for you, but the buyer's been there all day as far as we can tell."

I glance at Fender to gauge his reaction to Luna's words. She might be Riker's ol' lady, but she's also the president of the local chapter of the Devil's Handmaidens MC, and she definitely knows her shit. If she says the buyer and his men have been at the factory, they've been at the factory.

Fender's jaw clenches. "Motherfucker."

"We did a lot of legwork ahead of time," Greaser says. "We're good on the layout of the place, as well as the surroundings. This just means we have to be more vigilant."

My role in tonight's run is to stand guard at the back entrance of the factory, but I'm not sure that's even a possibility at this point.

"What're ya thinking, Prez?" I ask.

We met Luna and her girls in a deserted parking lot four miles away from the factory, and while this isn't a highly traveled road, I've had that feeling of being watched all day, and it's only intensifying the longer we stand out in the open.

"Nothing changes," Fender orders. "We go in, meet with Marco, finalize the deal, and get the fuck outta there."

"You still want us to go?" Luna asks.

"Oh yeah. It's common knowledge among the arms community that Marco is a sucker for sexy women and tends to prioritize his cock over his business. Having you all there just gives us an edge if we can throw him off his game even a little bit."

"This fucking sucks," Mousie, the DHMC VP gripes. "I could choke this guy out with my bare hands but instead I have to pretend I wanna choke on his dick."

"None of us like it," Riker snaps. "I certainly don't like my woman being a part of it, but it is what it is. When it comes to club business, we do what we have to do. That's not a new concept to you."

"Thanks, babe," Luna says lazily. "But I can handle my club. You stick to your own."

The skin on the back of my neck prickles with unease, and I glance over my shoulder toward the rocky hillside across the road. Nothing catches my eye, not that it would in the pitch-blackness of night.

"You okay, man?" Trainwreck asks me quietly. "You've been cagey all day."

"Cagey?"

"You're constantly looking over your shoulder, and you seem..." He shrugs. "I don't know. Off, I guess."

"You ever get the feeling like you're being watched?" I ask, voicing my concern.

"All the time," he admits. "But it's not surprising with what we do."

"No, I guess not."

"Get your shit together. If I've noticed, you can bet your ass Fender noticed. You don't want him leaving you behind because you can't get your head out of your ass."

"Luna, I'll leave it up to you if you wanna have one of your sisters take your van back to our clubhouse or if you want to have someone wait here," Fender says, pulling me back to the night's activities.

"Definitely not leaving the van or anyone here," she says. "If we have to make a quick getaway or scatter, I don't want to have to worry about a secondary location. We can just all meet back up at your clubhouse and go home from there."

"Sounds good." Fender scans the members of both clubs. "We all go in together and leave together. I don't give a fuck who you ride with, but ladies, please play the part you're here to play."

"Let's ride," Piston barks, and he's the first to mount his Harley.

There are more Soulless Kings than Devil's Handmaidens, so we aren't all paired up, and I'm grateful I'm a lone rider. It's bad enough to have one feeling I don't like, but to add to it a person on the back of my bike who has no business being there, and it's a little too much for me to handle.

Ten minutes later, we're standing face to face with Marco and four of his crew. He and Fender discuss the weapons to be included in the sale, but it's clear Marco is more interested in the women than the guns. His sleazy gaze keeps drifting from one to the next, his lecherous grin deepening with each of them.

"The price remains firm," Fender says after he finishes listing the guns. "And we only deal in cash."

"What about them?" Marco asks, nodding to the women. "Are they included in the sale?"

Fender's spine stiffens, but he keeps a mask of indifference over his features. "They're all taken."

"Oh, surely a deal can be made," Marco cajoles. He steps around Fender and strides right up to Mousie. I hold my breath, half expecting her to choke him out like she mentioned earlier. "I want her," he says as he taps her on the nose.

"I'm not so—"

"Not for sale, Marco," Fender barks, effectively shutting Mousie up. "Keep asking, and I'll take the goods to your competition and cut them a better deal."

Marco's second in command steps closer to Fender, his hand hovering above the 9mm Glock on his hip, but Marco holds his fist up, stopping the guy in his tracks.

"No need for nasty threats," Marco says as he turns around and faces Fender again. "We will accept the deal you're offering."

Discussion continues for a few minutes, and when we all walk out of the building, it's with the knowledge that in one week, we'll all meet again to exchange the weapons for the cash.

"Trainwreck and Royal, stay back and make sure we're not followed," Fender orders before we can mount our Harleys. "I don't think Marco had any others lurking around, but we can't know for sure."

"Sure thing, Prez," Trainwreck and I say at the same time.

Royal

Once they all leave, Trainwreck starts to walk away.

"Where ya going?" I ask.

"Might as well check the perimeter," he says.

As I quickly catch up with him, my nerve endings tingle, and I scan my surroundings for threats.

"Still acting cagey," he says.

"Shut the fuck up," I snap.

Trainwreck lifts his hands in mock surrender. "Sorry, man."

"How long do you think we need to hang around until we can deem the coast is clear?"

"Thirty minutes or so," he replies. "Fender will text when we can leave."

And sure enough, thirty-two minutes later, both our phones ping with a notification.

Fender: Head to the clubhouse if all good on your end.

"Looks like we can go," Trainwreck comments.

I flip my phone so he can see the screen and laugh. "Yeah, got the same thing. Prez is thorough, I'll give him that."

When we reach our bikes, I shove my phone back into the inner pocket of my cut and straddle Tyche. Both of us rev our engines, letting the sound reverberate through the night air.

"That never gets fucking old," he shouts over the rumble.

"Never," I agree. "Hey, I think I'm gonna take the long way back."

"I'll ride with ya."

"I'm good."

Trainwreck stares at me, assessing and making me feel like I'm being examined like a damn bug.

"Okay," he finally says.

I ride in the opposite direction as him, letting my mind race as the wind whips my face. I haven't been able to focus on anything since last night, and it's only gotten worse the more time that passes. Between the haunting story Paige told me about that picture, and the serious case of blue balls I went to bed with, I find myself questioning my life choices.

My money has always meant that things come easily to me, but it doesn't mean I haven't worked hard to get where I'm at. I graduated high school at fifteen and college at eighteen. My parents expected me to go to law school, but I was tired of spending every minute of my life with my head buried in books.

So I left.

It wasn't some tragic parting. Shit, there wasn't even an argument. My mother and father may have had expectations, but their biggest concern was my happiness. And being a biker makes me fucking happy.

BEEEEP!

The blare of a horn yanks me from the confines of my mind. I swerve to miss the car coming straight at me and skid to a stop on the side of the road. My heart pounds in my chest, and my breaths come in short, shallow pants.

Get it together!

There's a reason I chose the MC life. Sure, there's a lot at stake... actual life at times. But it allows me to be free from complications, free from thinking myself into an early grave.

Ignoring the way my stomach sinks at the thought, I

make a decision. I need free and easy. I need shallow and... fucking easy.

I need to stop obsessing over Paige and my crazy feeling of being watching and focus on someone like Alice.

Free, shallow, easy.

Chapter Eight

Fucking Royal and those eyes that won't leave my subconscious alone.

Paige

"Hey, boss, I'm gonna head to the country club."

I absently nod at George. He and I are working a couple's twenty-fifth anniversary party tonight, and it starts in a few hours. Standard practice is to arrive early, and usually, I'm the first out the door. But not today. Not at all the last few days, in fact.

"Want me to grab you something to eat on my way?"

"No, but thanks."

George comes deeper into my office and leans his fists on my desk.

"Okay, spill," he demands in a way that doesn't at all come across as an order.

"Nothing to spill."

"As my wife would say, bull dookie."

I snort out a laugh. "Bull dookie?"

He straightens with a grin. "Her version of bullshit," he

explains. "I don't know if I've ever heard her say 'shit', now that I think about it. She's got no problem with 'fuck' or 'damn', but 'shit' is where she draws the line."

"How did I not know this?"

"I see what you're doing," George says, waving a finger at me. "And I'm not falling for it."

"I don't know wh—"

"Paige, I like you, and I *love* my job, so I'm trying hard not to cross a line, but you're not making it easy." I narrow my eyes at him, but he just shakes his head. "I'm sorry, and if you want to fire me, go ahead, but I can't just sit back and watch you mope around any longer. You are always, always, raring to go and excited about the work, but not lately."

He's right. He's a thousand percent right. But I can't tell him why. I haven't even told Alice, and I won't until I have more. I just have to figure out how to get more.

"I've just got some personal stuff going on, George," I tell him, hoping like hell I sound convincing. It's not a lie, but it's a gross understatement. "I appreciate the concern. I really do. But I'm good."

He stares at me a moment longer before giving me a brief nod. "If you say so. But I'm around if you want to talk." He smiles. "That is, if you don't fire me for insubordination."

I chuckle. "I'm not gonna fire you." Leaning over the arm of my chair, I grab my purse, ignoring the fact that it holds the source of my stress. "But I will take you up on the offer of food. My treat though."

"Sounds good to me."

George and I drive separately so we can go home straight from the country club, and as I'm driving, my cell rings. Without thinking, I press the button to answer using the hands-free function in my car.

"Hello?"

"You're never gonna guess who called me," Alice says, and I swallow back my groan.

A pretzel-shaped knot forms in my stomach. "Who?"

"Guess."

"Alice, I'm on my way to an event, so the guessing game is gonna ha—"

"Royal," she squeals.

She squeals like a teenage girl who waited by the phone for months for her crush to call, and he finally called. And like the same teenage girl, I can't stop the barrage of memories of the boy's eyes.

Fucking Royal and those eyes that won't leave my subconscious alone.

"What did he want?"

"Believe it or not, he asked me to come to another party at the clubhouse."

"Alice," I snap. "You can't go back there. Those guys are dangerous."

My friend sighs. "I know they are but..."

An image of her sitting on her couch and chewing on her nails flutters into my head.

"But what, Alice?"

"Brock thinks it would be good for me to go."

You've gotta be kidding me.

"What could you possibly hope to gain by going to the party?"

"Blackmail, P." She sighs again, but this time it's more dramatic. "Brock thinks that I should take advantage of Royal's interest and maybe he'll tell me things."

"And what do you think?" I ask, wondering about that squeal.

"I'm gonna go."

Tell her. Tell her about your little escapade, about the pictures.

"I really wish you wouldn't."

"I'll be fine. It's not like he's gonna kill me with a room full of witnesses."

The restaurant where I'm meeting George is less than a block away, so I don't have time to argue with her. Alice is going to do what she wants, regardless of what I tell her. And really, there's not much to tell. I have pictures of a meeting. There's nothing criminal about a meeting.

"Listen, I have to go, but I'll call you later," I tell her. "Just... don't agree to anything before we can talk again, okay?"

"Yeah, okay. Brock and I are meeting at the bar later, but I'll keep my phone on vibrate. You know how loud it gets in there."

Thankful that she can't see me, I roll my eyes. "Got it. Later."

I disconnect the call just as I pull into a parking space. This is the restaurant of choice for all of my staff when we have time to go before events, and the staff know us well. We're greeted and seated immediately, and our drinks are placed on the table before we even have time to peruse the menu, not that we need to.

Thankfully George doesn't push for any more information, and dinner is pleasant. He talks about his wife and kids, pride in every word he utters. Guys like him are the reason I haven't lost faith in all of the male species.

When we arrive at the country club, it doesn't take us long to get inside and do any final prep of the cameras before our clients and their guests show up. We make use of the employee break-room to store our personal belongings, and I utilize the mirror in the employee bathroom to make sure I don't look as frazzled as I feel.

The anniversary party guests begin to trickle in ten minutes before the time that was on the invitation, and George is stationed near the door to capture pictures of the couple greeting each new arrival. I remain in the main room being utilized for socializing, and by the time everyone enters, I've managed to put worries about Alice out of my mind and focus on work.

As the celebration nears the end, I rush to take a bathroom break, and once I'm finished, I step back into the hallway only for my feet to become glued to the floor.

Walking out of the men's restroom is a man I recognize, one who I know nothing about other than where he was on Sunday night. And I've got the proof in my purse to prove it.

Chapter Nine

I don't know a man on the planet who likes feeling like a fool.

Royal

"Please tell me you only invited her and not that douchebag Brock."

After puffing on the joint between my fingers, I hold my inhale and pass it to Greaser, who takes a toke of his own. I was hesitant to tell any of my brothers that I called Alice but figured it would be worse if she simply showed up without any warning.

"Considering the vote on Brock in church yesterday," I begin, smoke curling out of my mouth as I speak. "No, I definitely didn't invite him."

When we have the open house parties, church is always held within a few days in order to discuss potential prospects I've identified. After his attitude, Brock wasn't exactly a candidate, but we voted anyway because the brothers felt strongly that he shouldn't be permitted on the property ever again.

"And what about Paige?" Fender asks from across the table. "Did you invite her?"

It takes every ounce of willpower I possess not to visibly react to his question. Even after making the decision to forget her, it's been difficult.

You dream about her.

Okay, it's been impossible. But I've been in impossible situations before and came out of them stronger for it. Take Flash's addiction for example. It wasn't easy to go to Fender about my suspicions, but Flash is clean and sober because of it, and I'm a better friend for not keeping my mouth shut.

"Nah, just Alice," I finally say.

Fender opens his mouth to respond, but then snaps it shut and shakes his head. I know what he's thinking, that I'm thinking with the wrong head, and I suppose he's not wrong. But I'm doing what I have to do in order to stay sane.

"How long are you gonna play this out with this bitch?" Greaser asks.

I shrug. "Don't know. Long enough to calm my cock, I guess."

"I remember those days," Fender comments.

"Like you need to calm your cock," Joker snorts. "You get pussy on the reg, Prez, and don't pretend you don't."

Fender grins. "That's true. Charlie does keep me satisfied."

"Pretty sure if you two fucked any more, you'd die of a heart attack," Riker taunts with a smirk.

"Sex or laying my bike down... those are the only two acceptable ways to go if you ask me."

"I don't know," I say. "One chick for the rest of my life? Doesn't sound all that appealing."

Liar!

"Don't knock it 'til ya try it," Joker says. "I never

dreamed of settling down, but Riley changed everything for me."

"Well, I'm not looking to have things change."

While the rest of them drone on about their sex lives, I rock my chair onto the back legs and pretend not to listen. In reality, I'm mentally taking notes because these fuckers are dirty as hell... and creative.

An image of Alice flashes in my mind, her painted red lips and her tight little body. I let my imagination run with it, and as I'm envisioning her dropping to her knees in front of me, the hair changes, as do the clothes. And when she tips her head back to grin at me, it's Paige's face I see, all makeup free and sinfully wicked.

I try to force my thoughts back to Alice but fail miserably. Paige is who wraps her mouth around my cock, sucking me to the back of her throat like a champ, and it's Paige who digs her fingers into my ass cheeks to pull me closer.

She swirls her tongue around my shaft as she slides toward the tip, and my balls tighten just before my cock spurts into her mouth.

"Ah, Royal, what the fuck, man?"

My arms flail as I try to stay upright in my chair, and when the front legs hit the floor, I find my brothers trying to disguise their smirks.

"What?"

"Dude, you were moaning," Joker says with a laugh. "Full-on fucking moaning like you were locked in some wet dream or something."

"Must be thinking about Alice," Fender comments, but his eyes are sharp, and I know he knows exactly who I was fantasizing about.

"Chick has an incredible mouth," I huff out, grateful Prez is keeping his true thoughts to himself.

"Uh huh," Greaser adds.

I shove away from the table and stand to walk away, but Fender rises too and leans across the table to grab my arm and stop me.

"I keep meaning to ask you," he begins. "Still getting the 'I'm being watched' heebie-jeebies?"

"Is nothing sacred around here?" I snap.

"Were your suspicions about Flash?" Riker asks.

"That's different."

"Trainwreck came to me because he's concerned," Fender says. "Same way you did about Flash. Not so different."

I glare at him for a moment. "No, no heebie-fucking-jeebies."

I yank my arm out of his hand and stalk toward the stairs to head up to my room. After stepping inside, I slam the door and flop down on the bed. I'm not upset with Trainwreck for saying something to Fender, and it's nice to know he has my back even if he has no clue why.

But I am upset with myself. The feeling of being watched ended, and I've convinced myself it was all in my head. As soon as I made the decision to stick to free and easy, it vanished, making me feel like a fool.

And I don't know a man on the planet who likes feeling like a fool.

* * *

"Any volunteers to stake out the factory prior to the buy?"

Trainwreck raises his hand, as does Gibson. I would

have, but Alice will be at the party, and I have no plans of cutting the night short to guard an empty building.

"That works," Fender says. "Take two prospects with you, that way you can cover all sides. I don't want to take any chances that Marco shows up even earlier than last time. We should be one step ahead, and we weren't."

"Now we know what to expect from him," Piston tacks on. "Do you want the DHMC there again?"

"I don't think it's necessary. Besides, I doubt Mousie will be able to keep her mouth shut a second time if Marco pulls the same bullshit."

"Dude, I'm still hearing about it," Riker says with a laugh. "She's driving Luna nuts with it, which means Luna is driving me nuts."

"I can imagine."

For the remainder of church, discussion focuses on Sunday. Plans are finalized, and everyone knows their role. Before Fender ends the meeting, he opens up the room for any other business.

After Flash reviews the club finances for everybody, we're dismissed. I'm almost to the door of the clubhouse when a hand lands on my arm to stop me from leaving.

"Are you really that pissed that you won't stake out the factory with me?"

I arch a brow at Trainwreck. "Do you really think I'm that childish?"

My friend sighs and shoves his hands in his pockets. "I'm sorry I told Fender about you being all cagey. But if your instincts were right and you were being watched, it could be related to the club."

"I know."

"And if it's club relat—" He presses his lips together for a moment and then narrows his eyes. "If you're not mad, why didn't you volunteer for the stakeout? We usually do those together."

"Jesus, you are not this stupid, T," I say. "I invited Alice to the party. I wanna fuck Alice. If I go to the factory, fucking Alice is out of the question because I'll have to leave the party early. So, I didn't volunteer."

"Oh. So you're not mad?"

"No, I'm not mad, dipshit. I was upset, but not at you."

"Then who the hell were you upset with?"

Why is it that when a man ties himself to a woman for the rest of his life, he turns into a gossipy bitch who gives a damn about feelings and shit?

I walk out the door with a nod for him to follow, and he does. We walk side-by-side to our bikes, and I ignore the weird looks Trainwreck thinks he's hiding. I know he doesn't understand why I'm dragging him outside to talk, but he will. As soon as I explain myself, he will.

"I'm pissed at myself," I blurt when I'm standing next to Tyche. "I'm pissed that I was so distracted by my gut, which was wrong, by the way, and when Fender brought it up in front of everyone, I felt like a total asshat."

"Wait a second," he says. "Why do you think your gut was wrong? And why the fuck would you feel like an asshat?"

"My gut was wrong because it just was." I heave a sigh when he simply stares at me with eyes full of expectation and confusion. "When I was riding home after the meet with Marco, I was so in my damn head that I almost ran headlong into a car. They honked, and I snapped out of it, but it hit me then that I was just in my head. I was obsessing about Paige when she's the last thing I need. I need easy. As soo—"

"And Alice is easy."

Royal

"Definitely easier than Paige," I deadpan. "I don't need an ol' lady, I need fucked. And as soon as I realized that, that sensation of being watched disappeared. And that, in turn, made me feel like an idiot."

"Okay, that's a lot of shit to unpack, but I'm gonna try." Trainwreck begins to pace. "First, you have to know that gut feelings shouldn't be ignored. I'm glad you don't think you were being followed anymore, but I wouldn't totally brush it off. Gut feelings are gut feelings for a reason."

"Yeah, but—"

"Not finished," he snaps. "Second, I get that you don't wanna get married, and I know exactly where you're coming from. I was all about pussy too... until I wasn't. Don't knock what you don't understand."

"I'm not kno—"

"Still not done," he barks, coming to a stop in front of me. "Third, and most importantly, why the absolute fuck are you just now mentioning that you almost died?"

Trainwreck crosses his arms over his chest and glares at me.

"Oh, I can speak now?" He nods. "I didn't say anything because I'm fine."

"Not the point. Soulless Kings don't have secrets. You don't hold something like that back, Royal."

"Well, you know now."

He simply shakes his head. "I'm gonna give you some unsolicited advice. What you do with it is up to you, but for the love of all that's holy, fucking take it."

"Okay, oh wise one. What's this advice?"

"Fuck Alice and then move on. She's trouble, brother." When I open my mouth to argue, he holds a hand up. "Gut feeling. Unlike someone, I don't ignore them. She's trouble. But your dick isn't gonna agree so scratch the itch and move on. It doesn't have to be Paige or even someone permanent. But move. On."

With that, he walks away, leaving me to ponder his words. I straddle my Harley, needing the open road while I'm once again, all up in my goddamn head.

Chapter Ten

Neither of us are most people.

Paige

"Okay, I'm here. Where the hell is the fire?"

I jump up from the couch and whirl toward the door to see Alice pulling it closed. As soon as I got into my car after seeing that man at the country club, I called her. Of course, she didn't answer, or even call me back. Apparently, I'm not as important to her as she is to me. When I woke up this morning and still hadn't heard from her, I texted her to get her ass to my loft ASAP and that it was an emergency.

That was six hours ago.

And six hours is a long damn time to sit and think and obsess and worry.

"What took you so long?" I demand, anger infusing my words.

"I'm sorry, it's been a long day."

Alice walks past me into the kitchen and grabs a bottle

of water out of the fridge. After unscrewing the cap, she tosses it in the trash and comes to the couch to sit.

"It's been days!" I shout. "I called you days ago, like you told me to by the way, and you never called me back."

"Okay, you need to calm down, Paige," she says as if she's annoyed with me. "You never get worked up like this."

I stomp to the narrow table near the door and snag my purse from it, and then stomp right back. Shoving my hand in, I grab the envelope of pictures and slam it onto the coffee table.

"This is the fire, Alice," I snap.

She stares at the envelope as if it actually will burst into flames at any second. "What is it?"

Throwing my hands in the air, I sit next to her and open the envelope to take out the pictures. "At that party last week, when I was kicked out, I was sta—"

"You're still mad about that?"

"Oh my God, Al, just shut up and listen to me," I bark.

Her eyes widen, and normally, I'd want to take back my harsh tone with her, but not today, not this time.

"Continue."

"Anyway, I was outside and overheard a phone call about some club business. I thought it would be a good opportunity to get the blackmail you and Brock need. So I went to the location where the business was and took pictures. I kept waiting for someone to notice that I was across the road, but no one did."

I start flipping through the photos. I've gone through them so many times that I organized them in some sort of order of importance in my mind. Location, vehicles, then images with people. Alice isn't looking at them at all. She's staring at me now like I've grown two heads.

"You actually did this?" she asks. "You put your life in jeopardy for me?"

The surprise in her tone shocks me into motionlessness, and my anger fades more than a little bit. "Well, I mean, yeah. You're my best friend."

Alice grabs the pictures from my hand and tosses them behind her on the cushion before she throws her arms around my neck. It takes me a moment before I hug her back because I'm not used to this from her. Alice doesn't show affection, not unless she's trying to get into a man's pants.

When she leans back, she folds her hands in her lap. "Sorry, I um..." She shakes her head.

"What's wrong?"

"Brock and I got into a fight," she admits. "I guess it's just nice to hear that someone gives a damn about me."

"Al, I've always given a damn."

Alice swallows. "I know. Even when you shouldn't have, you did."

"What's that supposed to mean?"

She tilts her head and gives me a weird look. "I'm not stupid, P. I know I haven't always been the friend you deserve. Hell, I made the fact that I *didn't* have sex on prom night more important than the fact that you did when you didn't want to. Don't think I don't know that you slept with Jordan because I pressured you."

"That was years ago. Forgotten and forgiven," I say.

It's not one hundred percent true. I will never forget, and there's a small part of me that will never forgive, but Alice has always been... Alice. I accepted years ago that I'm not the most important person in the world to her.

"And that's why I love you." She takes several deep

breaths. "But enough of that. Tell me about that club business."

The quick switch in topic doesn't surprise me. In fact, it's the first thing that hasn't surprised me since she stormed into my loft demanding to know where the fire was.

I take the time to fill her in on what I heard and what I saw even though it was barely anything. And then I tell her that one of the men Royal and the Soulless Kings met with was at the country club.

"Wait a minute... you saw him again?"

"Yeah, I mean, he didn't know who I was. We didn't even speak, but I froze. It scared the shit out of me."

"I can imagine."

"And now... Shit, Al, I don't know what to do. I want to help you. I hate that you're in danger. But how am I supposed to get blackmail? It's not like the Soulless Kings advertise their activities."

"That's what Brock and I got into a fight about," she admits. "Nothing has happened since we met with the police. I mean, wouldn't the club have done something if they knew we called?"

Hearing her voice one of my own worries, one of the many questions I've had since seeing that guy at the country club makes me feel less crazy.

"He's mad because there haven't been any threats or anything from the club?" I ask, incredulous.

"Yes," she cries, but immediately deflates. "No. I don't know." Alice fidgets with her hands as she tries to come up with the right words. "I think he's more pissed because I got an invite back, and he didn't."

Relief crashes over me like a tidal wave. I thought I was going to have to convince her not to go, but if she agrees that there isn't a threat from the club, this whole blackmail thing can end.

"Oh, I'm still going."

So much for relief.

"But why?" I demand. "Al, if there's no threat, there's no need to go."

"Maybe," she agrees. "But I want to go."

Leaning back against the throw pillow, I sigh. This is the Alice I know, the woman I'm familiar with.

"You want Royal." Most people would ask this with indignation, but most people don't know my best friend. It's not a question, and the only emotion in my tone is resignation. "He killed someone, Alice. You saw him kill someone."

Yet that doesn't stop you from wondering if he's all bad.

"I'm aware," she snaps. "Which is why I'm moving forward with the plan to blackmail him and his club. If I have to sleep with him to make it happen, so be it."

"And this is what Brock wants?" I ask, trying to come up with any reason that will matter enough for her to reconsider.

"Brock wants money, and he wants me to go. So yeah, I'm pretty sure he's fine if I fuck another man if that's what it takes."

"I can't believe this." I rise from the couch and begin to pace. "This is insane, Alice, and you know it. You showed up here scared out of your mind after witnessing a murder, and now that you may actually be given the gift of not having to worry about your own life, you're doing everything to make sure you're not safe. It's nuts. You're nuts."

Alice jumps up, her expression twisting into a mask of anger. "How is this any different than you following them on your own for some pictures? It's okay for you to put yourself in danger, but not me?"

"That's different," I counter hotly.

"How, P? How is it different?"

Throwing my hands up in the air, I stop in front of her and glare. "Because I didn't climb into bed with the threat!"

A furious flush seeps into her cheeks, and she looks at me as if I physically delivered a blow. She marches to the door and yanks it open, but before she leaves, she glances over her shoulder at me.

"Fuck you, Paige. Fuck you and the high horse you rode in on."

After she slams the door behind her, I slump onto the couch and hold my head in my hands. How is it possible to go from one extreme to the next so quickly? I was finally starting to feel hopeful that my best friend was going to be safe and that maybe, just maybe, I wouldn't have to spend so much of my energy on protecting her.

All hope is gone now though. Rather than decreasing my efforts to be the person in her life who actually gives a damn, I have to double them.

Most people would've cut ties with Alice a long time ago. But that's one thing my best friend and I have in common...

Neither of us are most people.

Chapter Eleven

Gut feelings are gut feelings for a reason.

Royal

The dopey grin on my face widens as I read the latest text from Alice. She's been texting me non-stop since I asked her to come to this party, and all of the messages have a sexual undertone to them.

Alice: I bought it just for tonight.

The words were preceded by a picture of Alice's reflection in a full-length mirror. She's wearing a G-string and a scrap of cloth I suppose is a bra but does very little to hide her nipples from me. The star pattern of material covers the peaks, but that's it. She has legs for days, and her skin is tan and her body tight.

I type a quick reply.

Me: Mmmm... nice.

Alice: Just nice? Maybe I should return it. I was going for more than nice.

Me: No! Don't return it.

Alice: So...

For someone who is clearly comfortable in her own skin, she sure needs reassurance. I have no problem giving it to her, but it makes me grateful that I'm not looking for anything beyond one night. I like confident women, independent women. And Alice doesn't seem to fit that bill completely.

Before I can reply, a notification pings. It's the alert sound I set up for when I receive texts from Fender, so I switch to the thread of messages with him.

Fender: Get downstairs. Now!

Alice forgotten, I race out of my room and down the steps, coming to a halt when I see Fender and Piston standing with Detective Harker, one of several cops the club has in their pocket.

"Royal, head into the meeting room. As soon as Gibson and Squirrel arrive, we'll meet you there," Prez orders.

I nod and make my way to the room where we hold church. My stomach churns with apprehension as I wait. There's only one reason Harker would be here, and that's to read us the riot act for some crime we committed that he or the others are having to cover up.

My mind flashes back to the night in the alley. I know Parker and Benny cleaned up the scene, and Parker's damn good. He knows what the law will look for and has never left anything behind before that could be linked to us.

So what the fuck is going on?

"Yo," Gibson says as he and Squirrel enter the room. "Any clue what this is about?"

"It's gotta be Tom and that drunk," Squirrel comments.

"That's all I can think of," I admit. "But I just don't know how that's possible. Parker is the best cleaner we've ever had."

The three of us sit there for another few minutes before our Prez, VP, and Harker walk in. None of them sit.

"What's going on, Fender?" Gibson asks.

"Should I call Lexi?" Squirrel asks.

Lexi is his ol' lady and the club's attorney. She got him off a bogus murder charge a while back and ever since, if there's trouble darkening our door as far as the law is concerned, Lexi jumps into the thick of it.

"Now, there's no need to get lawyers involved," Detective Harker says. "But we do have a problem."

"It seems there were witnesses that night in the alley," Piston says, frustration tinging his words.

"How?" I bark. "Who?"

Harker hooks his thumbs in his belt loops and rocks back on his heels. "We got a call that night stating that a couple had witnessed the murder from an apartment window above the alley. While your clean-up job was impeccable and the responding officer thought they were both a couple of alcoholics with a touch of crazy, the case was assigned to me to be sure."

"What case?" Fender asks. "You just said there's no evidence of a murder."

"There isn't. But when I saw the one witness's name in the report, I recognized it. I decided to do some more digging into the guy because you pay me good money to keep your club out of the limelight. And if my gut was right, this jackoff had connections that could spell trouble for you."

"And you're just now coming to us?!" I shout. "It's been wee—"

"Believe it or not, I have other cases to work," he snaps. "There are crimes being committed every day that I actually have to investigate."

"Was your gut right?" Piston asks.

"Yeah," the detective says proudly. I want to punch the smug look off his face, but I refrain. I might not like the delay, but he's here now, doing what we pay him to do. "He's got a cousin in the arms game. Pretty high level down south, but he shifted his operation here recently, so he's been on our radar. Your witness was listed in this guy's file as a relative. No priors or any hard evidence that he's involved in any of Marco's operations, but that doesn't mean he isn't."

"Did you say Marco?" Fender demands, his shoulders stiffening.

"I take it you know him."

"You could say that."

"I'm gonna regret telling you this, aren't I?" Harker asks.

"Depends," Piston says. "A huge problem is going to be eliminated from the community, and you won't have to lift a fucking finger. Some would be grateful."

Harker rolls his eyes. "Look, do whatever it is you have to do. But be careful. His cousin might not be a big player in the game, but that doesn't mean he won't become one."

"What's the cousin's name?" I ask.

Harker shakes his head. "Yeah, you're not getting that info. Not yet anyway. Let me talk to the guy and his girlfriend, feel them out as far as what they saw in the alley. Give me a chance to see if he's really a threat."

"If they saw what we did, they're a threat," I snarl, my thoughts twisting in my mind like a tornado.

Gut feelings are gut feelings for a reason.

Trainwreck's words taunt me. Maybe he was right. Maybe I was being followed.

"I get that, but I'm not gonna give you license to go kill someone else who might be completely innocent."

"Snitches aren't innocent," Gibson argues.

"But witnesses are," Harker snaps. "Give me a few days, and if I discover this guy is a threat, then you have my blessing to do what it is that you do."

Fender and Piston exchange a look before turning to me, Gibson, and Squirrel.

"Thoughts?" Fender asks.

"I want a name."

"Forty-eight hours."

"Twenty-four hours."

The three of us speak at the same time.

Fender focuses on our VP. "You were there with them that night," he says. "What do you want to do?"

"Forty-eight hours," Piston says without hesitation, then he turns to face Harker. "You've got two days to talk to them. But regardless of what you find out, you will give us the names of those witnesses. If you've deemed them a non-issue, we won't make a move. But we will keep an eye on them. And if they are an issue, they're as good as dead."

"I'm with my VP," Fender says. "But we also have to put it to a vote. If the club decides that's not the way they wanna go, then that's not the way we go."

Harker heaves a sigh. "That's the best I'm gonna get?"

"You know how this works," Squirrel says.

"Yeah, yeah I do."

Minutes later, a frustrated Harker leaves, and Fender calls an emergency church session. He only orders officers to be present, along with me, Gibson, and Squirrel since the vote he's calling pertains to the consequences of our actions.

When the vote is in favor of giving Harker forty-eight hours, like he was told we would, I'm not surprised. Fender and Piston are at the top of the food chain for a reason. They make smart decisions, and we're a better club for it.

But that doesn't mean there isn't a part of me that wishes the vote would've gone the other way. I want names. I want to take out the potential threat. I want this most recent act as a Soulless King to be in the past.

Killing isn't something I like to do, but it can't always be helped. And when it can't be helped, the last thing I want to do is worry about who saw what and who might be next.

Chapter Twelve

Sometimes good people do bad things.

Paige

"You're back."

I force a smile at Pony, who's covering the gate when I pull up to it. Exhaustion seeps into my bones, having had zero sleep last night as I agonized over what to do. I don't know what it says about me that I'm actually here, but that's a worry for another day.

"I am," I confirm.

Pony presses a button in the shack, and the gate swings open. "Try to actually follow the rules this time," he says. "No pictures."

"No pictures," I repeat.

Pony's chuckle is cut off when I roll up my window. I glance in the rearview mirror, and my anxiety ratchets up a notch when I see the gate close. There's no turning back now.

As I drive toward the Soulless Kings clubhouse, my

mind conjures up the conversation I had with George yesterday that set this whole fucked up plan into motion.

"I'm sorry, Paige, but I can't take it anymore."

I look up from the pictures on my computer, annoyed at being interrupted again. I've been editing these images since arriving at the studio this morning, and it seems as if my staff suddenly can't do a damn thing without me. George's brow is wrinkled with concern, and unlike earlier in the week, he doesn't wait before sitting in the chair across from me. And he doesn't beat around the bush.

"You bailed on a one-year-old's photo shoot this morning," he says flatly. "You never bail. And you've been holed up in your office and biting Evelyn's head off any time she tries to talk to you about something. She's out there crying now because you yelled at her for trying to confirm a booking for Monday. What the hell is going on?"

Guilt weighs me down at the reminder of my assistant rushing out of my office not five minutes ago.

"Noth—"

"No," he snaps. "That's not gonna work this time. I let it go the other day, but I can't do that again, boss. Something is wrong, and I want to help."

I stare at him a second before deciding that I need the help. I'm not stupid... I know I can't tell him exactly what's going on, but maybe I can talk in hypotheticals and get his opinion on what the hell I should do.

"Fine," I finally say, and his relief is visible in the way he relaxes into the chair and his face softens. "There has been something that's been bothering me."

"Okay. What is it?"

"I've got a friend who came to me with a problem last week, and I have no clue how to help her." I pause, giving him the opportunity to call me out on the lie that it's a friend,

but he doesn't so I continue. "We have a mutual acquaintance who witnessed something they shouldn't have, and they went to her when the police wouldn't help."

"Okay."

"Anyway, our mutual friend wants to blackmail the people she saw commit this crime because all she sees is dollar signs, and my friend agreed to help her. But then she met the person who committed the crime and even though she didn't like him, she's having trouble getting anything that can help with the blackmail. She tried following this guy but got nothing." George is staring at me intently, but he remains silent. "And now our mutual friend is going to try and get her own blackmail by sleeping with the guy. Don't get me wrong, I don't care who she sleeps with, but I also don't want her getting hurt. My friend is nervous about it too. She wants to help so our friend doesn't have to do anything so drastic, but she's also starting to wonder if it's all for nothing. I mean, she has no idea why the crime was committed. There could have been a good reason. She came to me for advice about what she should do. She thought about going to the cops but dismissed that idea because the cops supposedly ignored the crime to begin with. Then she thought about trying to follow the bad guys to get dirt on them. But she's also worried that, maybe she should just warn the bad guys because maybe they're not bad guys at all. You see, our mutual friend isn't always the best of people, and she can be selfish, and my friend is concerned that the whole thing is just wrong."

By the time I'm done rambling, my heart is pounding, and my breathing is labored as if I ran a marathon. George stares at me a moment longer before saying anything.

"In other words, your friend says she witnessed a crime and reported it, but the cops did nothing. She came to you

and asked you to help her find dirt on the criminal to use as blackmail to keep herself safe from their retaliation if they find out she witnessed the crime and to make money while she's at it. You agreed to help, but now you don't know if you should." When my brows practically touch my hairline, George smirks. *"C'mon, Paige. I'm not stupid."*

I swallow down my trepidation and nod. "Okay, fine. It's me."

"What crime did your friend witness? I mean, I'm sure I can guess, but just so I know I'm on the right track."

"She saw some people murder two men in the alley outside her apartment."

"And the cops didn't believe her when she called them?"

"That's what she said," I confirm, somehow at ease being honest with him. "She said that the criminals cleaned up the scene so there was nothing left as proof by the time the cops arrived."

"That's convenient," he muses. "But okay, let's say for argument's sake that all of that is true. She's worried that these men, who she watched murder two other men, are going to come for her when they find out she's the person who called the cops, right?"

"Exactly!" I exclaim. "And I think she has reason to worry."

"You think?"

"Well, I mean..." I sigh. "A little, maybe. This all went down weeks ago, and nothing has happened to her. No threats, no follow-ups from the police, nothing. If she were in danger, wouldn't something already have happened?"

"Maybe." George shrugs. "Maybe not. But what I'm more concerned about is what you hope to accomplish by helping to get dirt for blackmail. All that does is put you in danger."

"I know, but she's my best friend."

"You've got to be kidding me," he huffs. "Alice is the friend in question here?"

"No," I force out, but his arched brow tells me he hears the lie. "Fine. Yes, it's Alice."

"Aw, Paige. Alice is not a good friend to you. I know you grew up with her, and you're a great person so you want to do whatever you can to help, but I think you should back off."

"And what if something happens to her?"

George takes several deep breaths before responding. "I'm gonna play devil's advocate here, okay?" I nod. "What if there never was a crime to begin with, and all of this is just Alice's way of scoring a payday? I know she's dating that guy you don't like so maybe that's why. I don't know. I know it's hard to think of your best friend hurting you, but she's not doing you any favors by involving you. She's certainly not prioritizing your well-being like you are hers."

"Yeah, I thought about that."

"But even if she is telling you the truth, she doesn't have all the facts."

"Right, but..." It's my turn to shrug. "Murder is murder. They shouldn't be able to get away with it."

"And it's not your job to get justice. Just like it's not your job to protect Alice."

"I hear what you're saying, but wh—"

"You said you met this person, or people, right? The ones who did the killing?"

"Yeah. At a party."

"And what did your gut tell you when you met them? What kind of vibe did you get?"

Royal yelling at me fills my mind, but it's quickly replaced by his interest in the photo on my phone and his eyes. Mother. Fucking. Eyes.

"He's a dick, but I didn't get the impression that he recognized Alice or her boyfriend. And I wasn't afraid of him like I thought I'd be. None of them actually. I mean, don't get me wrong, they are assholes. And I know they're criminals. But I wasn't scared."

"Look, I can't tell you what to do," he says. "And I certainly don't want to give you advice that puts you in danger. But I will say this... sometimes good people do bad things."

Sometimes good people do bad things.

Sometimes good people do bad things.

As I pull up to the clubhouse and park my car in the same spot as last time, I repeat his words, over and over, for courage. George may not have told me to do specifically what I'm doing, but it's the only thing I could come up with based on our conversation.

I tuck my purse under the seat, climb out of the car, and stalk toward the entrance with an air of confidence I'm far from feeling.

Sometimes good people do bad things.

Chapter Thirteen

Curiosity killed the cat.

Royal

"I hope Squirrel has something soon."

Without being asked, Squirrel decided to do some digging of his own to see if he could track down who made the call to the police about the murders. He promised he would come tell Gibson and me at the party if and when he found anything.

"You and me both, brother."

I just hope Squirrel gets a hit before Alice gets here. Nothing kills the mood faster than club business.

The party isn't as packed as the last one, but it's still early. I'm not naive enough to think that every open house will yield potential prospects, but it is frustrating when none show up. Oh well. More time for my dick.

"Uh... why is she here?"

I follow Gibson's arm to see who he's talking about, and

groan when I see Paige standing just inside the door. Hopping off the stool, I shake my head.

"No clue, but I'm getting rid of her."

I stalk toward her, and the closer I get, the more confused I become. She's not dressed as casually as she was the last time, but she's definitely not one-night-stand material. Her jeans are tight, and her sweater hangs loosely off one shoulder. The heeled boots on her feet are a far cry from the clunkers she wore before, and when I reach her, I see the slight touch of blush kissing her cheeks. Her lips are glossy, but not with artificial color, and her eyes are accented by a smoky-gray shadow.

And fuck my life, my cock twitches at the sight of her.

"What are you doing here?" I ask, instantly regretting my harsh tone when her eyes slide closed and she takes a deep breath.

When she opens them again, she levels her gaze on me. The pulse point in her throat throbs erratically, and she swallows several times before speaking.

"I need to talk to you," she says, squaring her shoulders.

Curiosity slams into me, but Alice will be here any minute, and curiosity killed the cat. Or pussy in this case.

"What could you possibly need to talk to me about?" I ask.

Paige takes a deep breath and averts her eyes for a minute. I cross my arms over my chest and wait her out. Finally, she lifts her eyes back to mine.

"I have to tell you ab—"

"There's a lot of shit you have to tell us, isn't there Paige?"

I turn to see Fender, Gibson, and Squirrel stalking toward us with rage and disgust written on each of their faces in equal measure. And it's their expressions that seem to snap everything into place for me.

"It was you," I snarl after swiveling back to Paige.

"Wh-what was me?"

Fender grabs her arm when he reaches us and starts to drag her through the main room toward the hallway. I know where he's taking her, and I follow them, fury blurring my vision. The tiniest part of my brain screams at me to stop him, but I don't. I couldn't even if I truly wanted to.

She's a threat to the club. And she needs to be dealt with.

"What is happening?" Paige shrieks as she's being dragged. She struggles to break free from Fender, but Gibson grabs her other arm. "I didn't do anything. It's Alice!"

"What the hell is going on?"

I whirl around at the familiar voice. Alice is rushing toward me on impossibly tall heels, and for whatever reason, my only thought is how the fuck is she not toppling over.

"Royal, handle this," Fender barks, and then he twists to look at Piston over his shoulder. "Get everyone outta here, VP. Party's fucking over."

After issuing orders, he resumes his task of yanking a now stunned silent Paige toward the Nightmare Room.

"Royal, where are they taking her?" Alice cries.

"Did you know about this?"

"About what?"

I grind my teeth in an effort to not say too much. If Alice doesn't know her friend witnessed us murder two people, I don't want to give her that information. And if she did know, then she's as in trouble as Paige is.

And not someone you can sleep with.

Yet.

"I hate to do this, but you're gonna have to go," I tell her as calmly as I can manage given how much my blood is still boiling.

"Go? But you invited me. You asked me to come tonight, and I came."

"And you heard Fender," I counter, a little less calmly. "The party is over. I've got shit to do, and it doesn't involve you."

"Wow, um..." She runs a hand through her hair, and I can't help but wonder if it's a move meant to be sexy. It is, sort of. But the appeal is lost under the weight of her attitude. "I'm not leaving without Paige," she says with a stomp of her foot.

"I don't have time for this," I snap and turn to walk away. I look toward the bar and demand, "Parker, handle this for me."

Alice's protests, but I ignore her. I tune out the pissed-off rumbles of those who came to the party and welcome the outrage that floods my system the further down the hall toward the steel door I get.

When I reach the basement, I force myself to take several deep breaths before continuing to the entrance of the Nightmare Room. I stop and glance at the screen of the monitor that hangs outside the door, and the erection that died a slow death when I realized Paige is a threat to me, to my club, springs back to life at the image of her tied to a chair in only a bra and panties.

The door slides open and Gibson grins. "Glad you could join us."

"Has she said anything?" I demand as I step inside and the door closes behind us.

"Bitch won't talk," Squirrel snaps.

"She will," Fender says with a smirk. "In time, she will."

Clenching my fists at my sides, I move to stand in front of Paige. She's staring at the floor, and I can see her body trembling.

"We know you saw us," I finally say.

Paige doesn't move or react to my words in any way. Gibson and Squirrel stand against one wall, while Fender stands next to me.

"I suggest you start talking," he says.

She slowly lifts her head and glares at Prez. "I came to talk, but he..." She tips her head in my direction without looking at me. "*He* didn't want to listen."

"And what did you want to talk about?"

"Prez, why are we wasting our time with her?" I ask. "She saw us kill two people, went to the cops, and then waltzed her ass into our clubhouse and started taking pictures for fuck knows why. We don't owe her the chance to explain."

"Give me one good reason not to listen to my brother," Fender orders.

"I'll give you two."

"I'm listening."

Paige slides her eyes to me and narrows them. "I'll talk to you," she tells me. "And only you."

"No," Fender says flatly. "Absolu—"

"Royal," she says from behind clenched teeth, her dark eyes still boring into mine. "And only Royal."

"He's the one who wants to kill you and then ask questions," Gibson says from behind me. "You sure about this?"

The fear that was causing Paige to tremble seems to dissipate beneath what can only be described as a coiled snake ready to strike at the slightest instigation.

"I'm. Sure."

"Royal, if we walk out of this room, I need your word that she stays breathing."

"He won't kill me," Paige says with an assuredness I envy.

I let my gaze drop to her chest, then lower still to just above her panties. Taking my time and savoring the goosebumps that pop up on her flesh, I leer at her. When I slowly return my stare to her face, the light blush from her makeup has deepened to a sinful shade of crimson.

I smirk at my obvious effect on her. "Sugar, I wouldn't bet on that. You already saw me take lives, and I have to admit, the thought of taking yours is becoming more appealing by the second."

"Royal," Fender barks. "Your word."

I stiffen. "Fine. I won't stop her heart. You can go."

"Ah, you sure about this, Prez?" Squirrel asks.

"I'm sure. Royal knows there will be consequences if he goes back on his word. Far more detrimental consequences than some bitch seeing him commit a felony."

The three of them file out of the room, and the click of the door closing behind them seems to echo in the space. Paige flinches at the sound, and I grin.

"So, you told Fender you had two reasons we should let you live. What are they?"

Paige tips her head back, exposing the column of her throat, the swell of her tits that she tries to hide under her comfortable clothing. I adjust my cock while she's not looking, and mentally kick myself for absolutely loving the sight before me.

"Start talking, sugar," I demand.

She straightens, and the unshed tears in her eyes make the orbs seem extra-large. I refuse to let my very uncomfortable and unwelcome desire to comfort her take root, but it's more difficult than any human on the planet could imagine.

And more overwhelming than I care to admit.

"Talk!"

"A-Alice and Brock."

I lunge forward and practically touch my nose to hers. "Bullshit. I want the motherfucking truth."

"I-it is the truth. I swear," she says, stuttering. But she doesn't try to move away, she doesn't cave to her fear. She swallows it and continues. "Alice and Brock heard a noise through her apartment window. They went to see what it was and they..." She pauses, swallows again. "They watched you stab a man in the alley and one of your brothers strangle another."

"You're only confirming what I already know. You saw us."

"Your name was on the police report."

Squirrel's voice comes through the intercom, and Paige's eyes widen. The trembling starts again, and she grips the arms of the chair so hard her knuckles turn white.

"What?"

"He said your name was on—"

"I heard him!" she screams. Her chest heaves, and her breathing becomes labored. Paige tries to suck in air as she struggles against her bindings. The color drains from her face, and her trembling morphs into gut-wrenching sobs.

Without thinking, I scramble to untie the ropes holding her in place. When the first arm is free, she claws at her chest and neck, and when both arms are free, she uses the other one to claw at me.

I have no idea what is happening, but it's not at all the reaction I expected. And I can't help but wonder if we got this wrong.

How could we have gotten it wrong? Police reports don't lie.

Right?

"Paige, I need you to breathe," I say in an effort to soothe her as I capture her wrists in my hands. "Breathe for me, sugar."

She tries, but her struggle doesn't lessen. I let go of her wrists long enough to untie her ankles. As soon as she's free of the rope, she kicks out, and her foot connects with my chest. I fall backward, onto my ass, stunned.

Paige takes the opportunity to stand, her flailing arms wild, but the second she tries to lock her knees, they buckle.

With lightning-quick reflexes, I shift and dive forward to cushion her fall. The air is thrust from my lungs when her weight lands on top of me, not because she's heavy but because of the jolt to my body.

"I didn't see you," she cries as I wrap her in my arms.

I'm acting on instinct and gut reactions, and it's not lost on me that I've been fighting both so hard lately.

"I didn't..." Her breath hitches. "It wasn't me."

"Shhh, okay."

"H-how could she do th-this? It wasn't me."

Paige pounds her fists into my chest, and I let her. I absorb her pain the only way I know how.

"It wasn't me."

As I cradle her here in the Nightmare Room, thoughts swirl through my mind in a jumbled mess of unanswered questions. But one thought sticks. One thought isn't a question at all, and it fucking sticks.

Curiosity killed the cat.

Chapter Fourteen

There's a whole lot of good inside a person who would do what Royal did for me.

Paige

"Breathe, sugar."

As my mind and my heart shatter into a thousand tiny fragments, this murderer, this bad guy, this *man* holds me like I'm a piece of fragile glass. And all the while, when I should be scrambling away from him, when I should be fighting him tooth and nail to break away, all I want to do is crawl inside of him and let him absorb my pain.

How is my name on the police report?

You know how.

My brain is insistent even as my soul attempts to dismiss what I know to be true: Alice has been playing me all along. She and Brock.

"C'mon, Paige," Royal prods. "I need you to breathe with me. Deep breath in, and out. In and out."

I focus on his words, inhale and exhale with him, and it

isn't long before lungfuls of oxygen are no longer impossible. Sweat coats my skin, but the air around me seems to hold a chill, and I shiver.

"There ya go. That's good... real good."

I lift my head off Royal's chest and look into his eyes, letting myself sink into the goodness I see there, the concern of a virtual stranger. As I stare, Royal uses his thumb to wipe the tears from my cheeks. His touch is gentle, which is at odds with what I think I know about him.

Sometimes good people do bad things.

Finally, when the silence becomes so deafening I fear my eardrums will bleed from it, I force words to move past my lips.

"I didn't do it," I croak. "It wasn't me."

Royal releases a self-deprecating chuckle. "Yeah, I'm starting to get that."

"It doesn't change anything."

I startle at the voice filling the air and swivel my head to find the source.

"Intercom," Royal says. "It's just the intercom."

Embarrassment washes over me at the realization that, if there's an intercom, there's a camera. Melting down is bad enough in front of one person let alone a bigger audience.

"Paige, put your clothes on."

The order from the speakers is sharp, and I know the voice belongs to Fender. I want to refuse simply on principle, but that would be stupid. I'm cold, and half-naked is not exactly my favorite thing to be.

Royal slides me off his lap and lays back so he can reach my jeans and sweater with a stretch of his arm. When he hands me my clothes, I snatch them from his hand and hurry to put them on.

The longer I'm calm and able to breathe without

panicking, the more my fury at being dragged down to this room, stripped, tied to a chair, and accused of doing something I didn't do takes over every cell in my body.

Feeling stronger as the shock wears off, I stand and move to the door to start pounding on it.

"Let me out of here," I demand. "You can't hold me against my will. That's kidnapping."

I'm dimly aware of the shuffle of boots against concrete as Royal stands behind me, but it doesn't slow my assault on the door. My fists begin to ache and as I'm losing steam, the barrier slides open, and Fender is standing in front of me with his arms crossed over his chest.

"Tell me, Paige," he says. "Do you really think we don't fucking know this is kidnapping?"

"Prez, I think it's sa—"

"Shut up, Royal," Fender snaps, but he keeps his eyes trained on mine. "I don't know if that little scene was genuine or just another way you're putting your acting skills to use."

"I'm not acting," I tell him, my voice giving way to annoyance.

Fender arches a brow. "Ya know, I liked you. When I first met you, my gut told me you weren't a threat. But police reports don't lie."

I can't stop my very unladylike snort. Is this guy for real? Police reports are doctored all the time. Shit, I'm sure there are plenty out there that have been filled with nothing but lies in order to save their asses.

Like the one that landed me in this room to begin with.

"You disagree?" Fender asks.

"Yes!" I exclaim. "Sure, maybe police reports don't actually lie, seeing as they're a *thing*. But people lie, and it's people who make and write the police reports."

"Touché."

"Now let me go."

Fender looks past me to Royal, who I haven't heard or felt move closer. I glance over my shoulder at him and if I weren't in a precarious position, I might actually laugh at the confusion on his face.

"I thought you were the president," I say to Fender, and that snaps his attention back to me. "Isn't it up to you whether or not I can go?"

Fender growls, but it's not the sexy kind I read about in my books. It's low and threatening, and self-preservation kicks in forcing me back a step.

"Do you think it's wise to push me?"

"I just want to go home."

"And believe it or not, I want to let you. But wanting something doesn't make it the right thing."

"What do I have to do to prove that I wasn't who called the cops?" I ask, feeling defeated. "Because screaming and crying and being unable to breathe doesn't seem to be that magical thing. So please, tell me what the fuck I have to do."

"Can you prove it?" he counters.

That has me pausing because I don't have an answer, at least not one that will get me out of here faster. And then an idea sparks, and hope flares to life.

"Wait, aren't 911 calls recorded?"

"Yeah, so?"

I groan, wondering if he's being deliberately obtuse or if he's just this stupid. "If you listen to the recording, you'll know it wasn't me, right? Because the voice won't match mine."

"She's right," Royal says as he steps up next to me.

Fender and I both glare at him, although I'm sure for

very different reasons. He wasn't exactly jumping in to defend me earlier, so why is he helping me now?

But he helped you through whatever the hell that was earlier.

"Listen to the recording," I beg.

"Squirrel," Fender barks, and the other man steps into the doorway. "Can you get the recording?"

"It's like you don't know me at all, Prez," Squirrel jokes.

"Answer the damn question."

"Yeah, Prez, I can. Give me a few minutes."

Squirrel disappears and his footsteps tap against each step as he goes upstairs.

"Have a seat," Fender instructs with a nod toward the chair I was tied to.

Yeah, that's not happening.

"I prefer to stand."

I half expect him to force me into the chair, but he doesn't. Instead, Fender steps all the way into the room, and Gibson takes his place in the doorway. Fender leans against the wall, his arms still crossed over his chest, and he appears to not have a care in the world.

I whirl around and stalk to the opposite side of the room, acutely aware of eyes boring into my back as I do.

"You said you came to talk to me," Royal says quietly.

"I did," I confirm.

"What did you want to talk about?"

"Seriously?" I huff. "Now you want to listen?"

Royal shrugs. "What else is there to do?"

I stare at him incredulously. The Soulless Kings seem to have a serious problem with speaking without thinking. It boggles my mind, especially since I spend so much energy on measuring my words carefully in order to avoid hurting people I care about.

And how is that working out for you?

"I'll talk when you admit that you're wrong about me."

Silence ensues, and it drives me insane because silence gives my mind the freedom to think without distraction. And what I'm thinking about only causes me pain.

How could Alice do this to me?

Rather than allowing myself to spiral down that dark pit of despair, I count. And when Squirrel reappears, I freeze on four thousand nine hundred and twenty-eight.

"Well?" I ask when he doesn't say anything.

"The recording is gone," he says to Fender.

My head spins, and I can feel the blood drain from my face, no doubt leeching all the color with it.

"That's not possible," I argue.

"It's not common," Squirrel concedes with barely a glance in my direction before looking at Fender. "Which is why I called Harker and asked him about it."

"Harker?" I ask. "Who's Har—"

Fender holds his hand up, and I press my lips together. "And what did he have to say?"

"He said he scrubbed the recording from the system the day after the call," Squirrel explains. "Said he figured it wouldn't be good for us if he didn't."

"The fucker's thorough, I'll give him that." Fender faces me. "So, any other ideas on how you can prove it wasn't you?"

"Ah, Prez, there's more," Squirrel tells him. "Turns out, the police report that I got from the system didn't contain all of the information from the call."

"Jesus," Fender mutters as he scrubs his hands over his face. "Explain."

"Apparently, Harker removed a name from the report

after meeting with us earlier today, the one connected to Marco."

"Who's Marco?" I ask.

"And I'm guessing, based on the disgust on your face, he refused to give you that name since we already gave him forty-eight hours to do his own digging."

"You got it."

"I'm starting to think Harker needs removed from our payroll," Gibson gripes. "This is bullshit."

"Agreed." Fender turns to me. "Any other ideas? Because so far, you haven't been able to prove that you didn't call."

Once again, I'm wracking my brain for something, anything, to get me out of this mess. I know I should just come clean about the blackmail, show them the pictures that are in my car, try to plead my case that I had no choice. But I hold that information back because they're not gonna believe a damn thing I say as long as they think I'm the snitch.

And then it hits me like a freight train.

"My loft," I blurt.

"Your loft?"

"I've got proof at my loft."

"What proof?"

I shake my head. "No. I'm not telling you, but I'll show you." I slide my eyes to Royal and then back to Fender. "Well, I'll show him." I tilt my head at the man who held me when I was losing my shit. "I'll show Royal."

Fender appears to think it over for a minute before finally giving a curt nod. "Fine. Royal, take her to her loft and see whatever it is she thinks will clear her. And then get both your asses back here."

"What?" I snap. "No, if I prove I didn't do this, I'm not coming back here."

Fender stalks toward me, his face a mask of indignation. "If I say you come back here, you come back here. If you prove your innocence, great. But that doesn't mean I won't still have questions."

"Then ask your questions now!"

"Proof first," he snarls. "Then questions." He turns away, effectively dismissing me. As he walks out the door, he calls to Royal, "Better get going. We've got other shit to deal with in a few hours."

Squirrel and Gibson follow their president, and Royal turns to face me. "C'mon, let's go."

My chest heaves with apprehension. What the hell am I doing?

Trusting your gut.

My instincts tell me that George is right and sometimes good people do bad things. It's also telling me that there's a whole lot of good inside a person who would do what Royal did for me despite his hatred.

You can do this. You were willing to put your life on the line for Alice, so why are you balking at doing whatever it takes to save yourself?

I push off the wall and stride past Royal. His chuckle sets my nerve endings on fire, and not in a way that's all that unpleasant. Rather than getting mad at my reaction to him, I focus on the rage I have for Alice. I focus on the task at hand: proving I'm not the bad guy.

"Well," I call over my shoulder once I hit the bottom of the steps. "Let's go."

Chapter Fifteen

Crazy, crazy, crazy.

Royal

"Well, let's go."

I shake my head and race out of the Nightmare Room to catch up to her. It's not often a woman stuns me into inaction, but Paige has taken me through a gambit of action and inaction since the moment I met her.

"Where the hell is the fire?" I ask when I reach her side.

She freezes mid-step at my words and glares at me for a second before continuing.

"So it's okay for you to rush, but not me?" she snarks.

"How am I rushing?"

"You rushed to judgment, that's for damn sure."

I don't have a response to that, so I say nothing. She's right. I hadn't even heard the words come out of Squirrel's mouth that he'd found her name on that police report. I took one look at his face, at Fender's face, and snapped.

Once we reach the main room, I grab her arm in an effort to control the situation. She seems to be cooperating, but there's still a matter of proof that she's not a threat, and I wouldn't be doing myself, or the club, any favors if I lose sight of that.

Paige tries to yank her arm out of my hold, but I tighten my grip, refusing to let her go. We walk across the room, and just as we're a few feet from the door, movement catches my attention out of the corner of my eye.

"Oh my God, you're okay!"

Paige twists toward Alice so fast she almost stumbles, but I hold her steady.

"What are you still doing here?" I demand then look past Alice at Parker. "I thought I told you to handle this?"

"I'm not something to be handled," Alice snaps with a huff. "I wasn't leaving without Paige."

Paige stiffens, and her eyes darken. Her adrenaline kicks in and she pulls free of me to launch herself at Alice. She grabs fistfuls of hair and throws Alice to the floor with a feral yell.

"You fucking bitch!" she screams as she straddles her friend—ex-friend?—and hauls her arm back to punch her.

Parker and I react simultaneously, me going for Paige and he for Alice. I manage to stop the attack before any blows are delivered, but the woman in my arms is flailing against me, using all her strength to extricate herself from my hold.

"Get her downstairs," I order Parker, and watch for a moment as he drags a now crying Alice to the same place Paige was just released from.

I don't know what her deal is in all this, but I know neither of them are gonna be out of our sight while we figure it out. Paige said Alice and Brock are behind whatever the fuck is going on, and as much as I want to argue the point, as much as I want to have been right in my decisions, I can't deny how hard she's fighting to prove herself.

Anyone willing to stand up to a Soulless King when it'd be wiser for them to shut up deserves the opportunity to prove themselves. If Paige had begged, if she's whined and pleaded, I might feel differently. But she didn't, not really.

And her breakdown was real. It had to be real. I've seen a lot of movies and never have I seen a performance that good.

Paige continues to struggle against me, so I bend to scoop her up and toss her over my shoulder. She pounds my back and kicks her legs, but when I pinch her ass to shock her into stopping, she does.

"I hate you," she bites out.

"No, sugar, you don't," I say, remembering the way she practically crawled into me in the Nightmare Room. "You want to, and maybe you should. But you don't."

"I hate you," she repeats with less heat.

"Okay."

I carry her to the passenger side of her car before setting her on her feet. Paige immediately turns away from me and rather than acknowledge that, I reach past her to open the door for her.

"Get in."

"No."

"Listen, you wanted me to go see whatever it is you have at your loft, and I'm doing my best to do that. So get in the damn car."

She tries to move past me, but I snake my arms out to block her in. Paige narrows her eyes. "I'm driving."

"Like hell you are."

When she opens her mouth to argue further, I do the

very last thing I should in this situation. I do the dumb thing, the asshole thing, the incredibly fucking... delicious thing.

I kiss her, tracing the seam of her lips with my tongue and begging for entry.

And it has the desired effect of shutting her up, but my chest takes another beating as she shoves me away.

"What the fuck was that?" she demands as she swipes her mouth with her arm.

The dome light from her car casts a dim glow, but despite the darkness, I see that her pupils are dilated. I see her nostrils flare and her chest expand as she sucks in a breath. Her words are angry, but her body is hungry.

"Get. In."

Paige hesitates, and I brace for an argument, but after a moment, she whirls around and climbs in. She pulls the passenger door to slam it, and I take my time walking around to the driver's side.

After taking a deep breath, I open the door and get in, cursing when my knees hit the steering wheel.

"I'm shorter than you, dumbass," she grumbles.

"No shit," I snap as I raise the wheel and shift the seat back as far as it'll go so I don't feel like a goddamn pretzel. I hold my hand out, palm up. "Keys."

"It's a push-start. Press the brake," she instructs.

When I do, she presses the button to the right of the steering column, and the engine purrs to life. Paige rattles off her address, and I enter it into the GPS on my cell.

"You know I can tell you how to get there, right?"

"And how am I supposed to know you're not gonna take me straight into a trap?"

She flaps her hand dismissively. "Suit yourself."

The ride is quiet. Paige stares out the window as I

drive, and I try like hell not to feel claustrophobic in a cage. It's not like I never ride in vehicles other than my Harley, but I much prefer Tyche and the open road to being boxed in.

When I pull up in front of Paige's building, I put the car in park, and she's out on the sidewalk before I can even open my door. She walks around to the driver's side and shoves past me when I step out. When she straightens, she slings her purse strap over her head.

Paige takes a step to walk away, but I reach out and stop her.

Is she always walking away from people? Does she like to be manhandled to force a conversation?

"I would've gotten that for you," I tell her. "All you had to do is ask. You coulda saved yourself a few steps."

"Pot meet kettle."

"Excuse me?"

"You wanna call me out for not asking for something and just taking it yet you didn't even stop for a single second to ask me what was going on before letting your *brothers* haul me to a room and strip my clothes off in order to take what they wanted." Her words are rushed and heated. "Coulda saved yourself a few steps too."

It's not like they stripped and raped her or anything. Hell, she wasn't even naked. Don't get me wrong, I get what she's saying, but does she have to make it sound worse than it was?

And even as I wonder about that, I know I'm unable to refute her logic.

With a deep breath to control my temper, I guide her to the door. Surprisingly, she doesn't struggle. We ride the elevator up to the third floor, and when we step into the hall, Paige digs through her purse for her key.

"This is a cool building," I observe, trying to keep things light.

"It is."

After unlocking the door, she pulls it open and moves inside. I follow, despite not being invited. Not that I was gonna give her a choice in the matter, but an invite would be nice.

Now you're just thinking crazy.

While Paige goes to the island that acts as an anchor between the living and kitchen areas and dumps the contents of her purse out, I take a moment to take in my surroundings. The loft is not at all what I pictured for her home, but somehow it perfectly suits her.

There are walls of exposed brick, as well as an accent wall that's painted a dark gray. The painted wall is filled with large unframed artwork, and when I move closer, I realize they're pictures. They're also the only spots of color in the space other than a few throw pillows and tasteful accent pieces.

"Did you take these?" I ask as I study them.

Some of the pictures feature people, while others are images that show scenes only made more beautiful by the lighting. Take the picture in the center of a field full of sunflowers. The picture was clearly taken at night, but the way the moonlight plays on the yellow and orange of the petals is incredible. The brightness of the color is silhouetted against the dark, and it's almost as haunting as it is stunning.

And now I'm thinking like a pussy.

"Does it matter? Will that somehow magically change your opinion of me?"

My opinion is already changing. It's been changing like

a goddamn chameleon changes colors since the moment I heard your voice.

Shoving my hands in my pockets, I turn to face her. "No," I tell her honestly. "It's just... they're good. Really good."

She whips her head up from the envelope in her hand and stares at me with wide eyes. "Um, thanks."

"You're welcome." I close the distance between us, and she backs up a step. "So, this proof..."

"Right." She swallows, but then seems to shake herself out of whatever stupor I put her in. "Gotta get my laptop."

Paige dashes toward the hall, and I follow... again. Seems I'm destined to follow her.

Crazy, crazy, crazy.

She grabs her laptop from her nightstand and sits on her bed before opening it. I lean against the doorway with my arms crossed, forcing myself not to imagine what it would be like to sit next to her on the mattress, what it would be like to strip her completely bare and lay her back before ravishing her.

"Here it is," she says as she jumps up and flips the computer around in her hands to show me. "See the timestamp?"

The video on the screen is from a security feed, that much I can tell because it looks like every other security footage I've ever seen. The difference is it's a clear image. I watch as Paige unlocks her door from the hallway, the camera pointing down from an angle.

Funny, I don't remember seeing a camera when we arrived.

I slide my eyes to the timestamp, and the date and time displayed line up with the night in the alley. If Paige was here, at her loft, there's no way she could've been the witness who called 911.

"You didn't call," I say pointlessly.

"That's what I've been trying to tell you."

Exasperation clings to her words, and she crosses back to the bed to drop her laptop onto it. When she faces me again, Paige is fidgeting with her hands, and my stomach drops. She might not have called, but she's holding something back, something she fears telling me.

"Why did you come to the clubhouse to talk to me, Paige?"

She takes a deep breath, then another and another before responding. "I didn't call. I didn't see anything. But Alice did. She lives in the apartment above the bar by that alley, and she and Brock saw what happened."

While her shoulders sag slightly, as if a weight has been lifted, she's still fidgeting, still holding something back.

"What else did you want to tell me?"

"I, um..." She swallows and then clears her throat. "I... they asked me to help them, after they called the cops. They had this plan to blackmail you and the club for hush money." I open my mouth but before I can get a word out, she rushes to add, "They thought you all would track them down and hurt them, so I agreed to help. I only wanted to protect Alice because she has no one else in her life that gives a damn." Tears fill her eyes. "Turns out she played me. She used my name when she made that call and then lied to me about it, about everything. Hell, I don't even know if you actually killed two men. I don't know anything anymore."

By the time she stops talking, tears are streaming down her cheeks. I don't correct her words about not knowing if we committed the murders because she *does* know. We all but told her when she was in the Nightmare Room. But that's not what's important right now.

I stride across the room and pull her into my arms, that damn need to comfort her coming back full force.

"So that's why you were taking pictures at the party," I say, putting all the pieces together, and she nods. "Okay, well, you deleted those, so no damage done."

Fender would kick your sorry ass if he heard you say that.

Paige pulls away and hiccups as she looks up at me with large eyes. "There's more."

I groan because of course there is. I might not know much about this woman, but she's stubborn and damn determined. If she was trying to protect her friend, it doesn't surprise me one bit that she has more confessions to make.

"Okay. What else?"

"I overheard a conversation after you kicked me out that night. And I may have followed up on it."

"What do you mean?"

"The club business you had the next day, at that bottle factory... I was there."

"Are you nuts?!" I shout, unable to control the burst of anger coursing through my veins. "You coulda been killed!"

"Well, yeah, I know," she admits, confusion in her tone. "But I didn't have a choice, Royal. I had to get evidence. I had to keep my friend safe."

"There's always a choice, sugar," I snap.

"If one of your friends, your *best* friend, or one of your brothers in the club even, needed you to do whatever it takes to keep them safe, would you do whatever it takes? Regardless of the consequences or danger you might bring on yourself, would you do what had to be done? Or is there a line you're not willing to cross for the people you love?"

Well, fuck.

Chapter Sixteen

I'm not your ol' lady so you owe me no explanation or loyalty.

Paige

There isn't a line in the world I wouldn't fucking cross.

Royal's words play through my mind as he drives us back to the clubhouse. I tried to convince him to let me stay at my loft, that the club had nothing left that they need from me, but he was having none of it.

He's loyal, I'll give him that. His only argument for refusing to leave me behind was that his president gave him an order, and he was going to follow it.

After I told him about the bottle factory, and he made his admission about having no lines, I calmed down. I can't explain it, but I got the sense that he understood why I did what I did, that he respected me for it even.

"You're quiet."

Because I don't know what to say.

I nod, but don't look toward Royal. He's seen sides of

me in the last few hours that I didn't even know existed, and none of them were flattering.

Although...

In the last few hours, Royal has also looked at me like no man ever has before. He stared at me with lust in that awful room, even though he tried to make it seem dirty and lecherous, it... wasn't. And then there were the few seconds after I shoved him away from kissing me.

I still don't know why he did that, aside from wanting to shut me up I suppose. It shut me up. And turned me on and made me mad and sent heat curling through my stomach toward my—

"I know how to shut you up, but I don't know how to get you talking."

I twist in my seat and stare at him.

"What?"

"So, you're *not* lost in la-la land."

"Of course not," I snap.

Royal's grin makes me want to smack him, but then he reaches across the center console and lifts my hand, and my brain short circuits.

"Are you okay?" he asks, genuine concern in his tone.

"I'm fine. Why wouldn't I be?"

"Oh, I don't know. You're in a car with a man you swear you hate, a man you were trying to save your friend from, and said man is driving you to be near other men who forced you into a scary room and tied you to a chair."

That about sums it up.

"And then there's the matter that your best friend betrayed you, and you're five minutes away from facing her."

Oh yeah, let's not forget that little nugget of fucking information.

"I don't hate you," I blurt, unable to think of something else, *anything* else, to say.

Royal chuckles. "I know."

"Then why would you say I do?"

"Because I wanted to hear you say you don't."

"Oh."

Royal was right. Five minutes later, he's parking my car near the clubhouse entrance. The only vehicles in sight are motorcycles, but I don't know if that has more to do with the fact that Fender sent everyone from the party packing or the fact that it's the middle of the night.

We both silently exit the car, and he leads me inside. I brace myself for the same treatment I received earlier, and anxiety sets my pulse racing when Fender starts walking toward me from the bar. I try to take a step back, but Royal rests his hand on my lower back to hold me in place.

He leans over and whispers, "You're stronger than that."

I lift my eyes to his and see the truth in them, the belief and respect. It bolsters my confidence, giving me the courage to square my shoulders and face Fender.

"Paige," Fender says when he reaches me.

Belief and respect. Confidence and courage.

"I told you it wasn't me."

"You did," he concedes. He slides his stare to Royal for a moment before returning to me. "I don't say this often, and to be honest, I don't feel it often, but..." Fender rubs the back of his neck, clearly uncomfortable. "But I'm sorry. We were wrong, and I'm sorry."

Tilting my head, I frown. "Are you sorry you were wrong, or sorry for how you treated me while being wrong? Because there's a difference."

Fender huffs out a laugh. "Not many people stand up to

me, ya know. But the people that do tend to be the ol' ladies around here."

"Ol' ladies?"

"Significant others, wives, girlfriends, life partners... whatever you want to call it," he clarifies. "It's always the women who don't hold back, who speak what's on their mind no matter how scared they are of me or how I'll react."

"You say that like it's a bad thing," I comment, wondering where this is going.

"Royal, I like her. Don't fuck this up."

Fender turns away, but my next words stop him.

"Where's Alice?"

He looks over his shoulder. "With the information you gave Royal, where do you think?"

"I want to talk to her."

Fender sighs and slowly spins back around. "No."

"I want to talk to Alice."

"I heard you the first time," he says with exaggerated patience. "No."

I march up to him, not an ounce of fear holding me back despite it being very present. "I am going to talk to Alice," I snap. "You can either let her go and bring her to me, or I'll go down there to that, that—"

"Nightmare Room," Royal says from behind me.

"Thank you. That's a horrible name, by the way," I say with a shake of my head. "But that's beside the point. If you don't bring her to me, I am going to her."

Fender arches a brow. "The answer *was* no, it's *still* no, and it *will always* be no."

Recognizing that he's not going to give in to my demands, I switch tactics. Maybe I can use a little of the logic I used with Royal.

"Can I ask you something, Fender?"

"Sure. But make it quick. I've got work to do."

"If someone you trusted, someone you thought you knew like the back of your hand betrayed you, hurt you in ways that were previously unimaginable because of who they are, would you want a practical stranger to ask questions and demand answers, or would you insist on talking to them yourself? Would you insist on seeing them, on hearing from *them* what their reasoning was?"

Fender stares at me for a moment before throwing his head back and laughing. I fail to see the humor in the situation, but apparently, I'm alone in that because when I look over my shoulder at Royal, he's laughing too. Although he's doing a much better job at controlling it under my scrutiny.

So much for using the same logic.

"There's nothing funny about any of this," I snap, annoyed that they're not taking me seriously.

"No, there really isn't," Fender agrees when he sobers.

"Ten minutes?" Royal asks.

"Ten minutes. And you're there the entire time," Fender says. "You can send Parker back up for now. He's keeping an eye on her."

Royal grabs my hand and drags me toward the hallway.

"What just happened?" I ask him.

"Sugar, you just broke the president of a one-percenter motorcycle club," he replies with what sounds a lot like awe. "You won. Don't question it."

"Oh."

Royal doesn't let go of my hand, even when it has to be obvious that I'm not gonna run. But when we reach the basement, he does squeeze it.

"You sure about this?" he asks.

"No."

"You don't have to talk to her."

Royal

"Yes, I—"

"Hey, Royal," Parker says when we near the door to the Nightmare Room. He's sitting on a folding chair and watching a monitor hanging on the wall. "What're you two doing here?"

"Head on upstairs, Prospect," Royal commands.

"Uh, okay."

Parker stands and starts to walk down the hall toward the steps but stops before ascending.

"I gotta say, Alice's body might be bangin', but she's annoying as fuck, man. I'm glad your plans to fuck her got derailed tonight."

Royal groans but says nothing. He does glance at me though, with a look that resembles shame and remorse.

"It's fine," I tell him. "I know guys want her. They always want her."

"It's not like that," he says.

"And I'm not your ol' lady so you owe me no explanation or loyalty. Now, can you open the door? Please?"

Royal does as I ask, and when there's no longer a barrier between me and my best friend, my betrayer, I lose my shit.

I rush toward Alice and yank her out of the chair by her hair, enjoying the crack of whatever bone hits the concrete floor. I don't know if I actually broke anything, but I don't really care either.

"You motherfucking, cock-sucking, back-stabbing bitch!"

Chapter Seventeen

There's a first time for everything.

Royal

The sea of red lights in front of me pisses me off, but I hit my brakes and follow my brothers into the same lot where we met with the Devil's Handmaidens last time we met with Marco.

"What are we doing?" I ask after pulling the van up next to Greaser's Harley.

"Don't know. Prez stops, we all stop."

Fender gets off his bike and walks to stand between the van and the others.

"Prez?"

"I just got a text from Harker," he says. "I put a call into him before we left to get confirmation that Alice really didn't know about Marco."

"Why?" I ask. "It doesn't change anything. Marco still dies."

"He does," Fender confirms. "It doesn't change

anything about what we're doing. But I needed to know if she was aware of him or not because she's back at the clubhouse with my woman, and all of yours."

"Curly, Flash, Pony, Craze, and Chaser are there," I remind him. "And the prospects. They're fine."

"I'm sure they are, but they need to know who they're dealing with."

The hair on the back of my neck stands on end at his tone. "And who exactly are they dealing with?"

"Definitely not the person Paige thinks is her best friend," he says cryptically. He pulls out his phone, and based on the way his fingers are flying over the screen, he's sending a text to those back home. "Alice not only knows about Marco, but she and Brock have been arrested in various states for crimes committed for Marco."

"How the fuck did Harker not know that before now?" I demand.

"No clue, but I promise, we will be asking that exact question once we're through all of this shit." Fender shoves his phone back into his cut. "I know they can all handle themselves, but it doesn't hurt to be extra cautious."

I don't understand his sudden concern. He's always trusted the brothers to protect the women, to protect the clubhouse. And now he doesn't.

No, that's not even right. I don't think it's about trust. Something else is going on, something he's not telling us.

Fear grips me at the possibilities of what that might be. I lift my cell off the dash and pull up my texting app to send one of my own. And I ignore the voice in my head telling me I have no right to worry about Paige.

I'm worried and that's that. Fuck it.

Me: B careful around Alice. Worse than we thought.

I stare at the screen, waiting on a reply, but by the time Fender's ready to pull out, I still haven't gotten a response. Sighing, I slide my phone into my pocket so at least I'll feel the vibration when—if—she responds.

After Paige talked to Alice, she crashed in my room at the clubhouse. I wanted to crawl into bed next to her, only to sleep, but Fender called church to rehash the plans for Marco and to discuss what we learned from both Paige and Alice.

By the time she woke up, it was time for us to ride out. I asked her to stay at the clubhouse, at least until I got back so I could take her home, and I have to admit, I was a little shocked that she agreed.

She's sleep deprived. That's the only reason she's still there, right where I want her.

"Let's ride," Fender shouts.

It only takes another two minutes to get to the bottle factory, and when we pull into that lot, I see Marco's dark SUV and no sign of Trainwreck, Gibson, or the prospects they brought with them to stake out the building.

I park the van as close to the entrance as I can, knowing we have to lug in the crate of weapons Marco thinks he's buying today. We could've brought an empty box, but it was agreed that having the extra firepower wouldn't hurt.

Fender signals for all of us to gather at the back of the van. "We go in, surround Marco and his men as quickly and inconspicuously as possible, and we take them all out. Trainwreck and Gibson are out back and know to enter only if they hear the code word. These walls are thick, and even with the broken windows, you'll have to yell fucking loud for them to hear you. Any questions?"

"Are we really using 'twatopotamus' as our code word?" Joker asks.

Fender shrugs. "This is what we get for letting our ol' ladies pick our code words. Besides, it was Riley's turn. If you've got a problem with it, take it up with her later."

"Maybe it's time we change that rule," Riker suggests with a groan, no doubt remembering that the last time it was Luna's turn, she chose 'baloney pony'.

"Bring it to a vote," Fender barks. "This is not the time."

"Understood," Joker and Riker mutter simultaneously.

"Grab the weapons, and let's go."

Greaser and I get the crate out of the van, and as I'm about to close the door, my cell vibrates in my pocket. I brace the load on my knee to take out my phone and look at it.

Paige: Ugh... ur killing my buzz... she's still in NR.

I tap the microphone icon so I can reply via talk to text.

"Sorry, sugar. And good."

"Sugar?" Greaser arches a brow at me.

"Stuff it," I snap, shoving my phone back into my pocket and lifting the crate with both hands again.

Greaser shakes his head with a laugh. "No judgment here, man."

"What're we judging?" Piston asks when we join them back at the door.

"Let's do this," I say to avoid the question.

We enter the factory and walk with purpose down the hall leading into the main room. Marco and the same men who were with him last time are standing dead center. They're doing their best to look intimidating but failing miserably.

Not much can intimidate men who have what we have in this giant box.

"Marco, nice to see you again," Fender says jovially.

Marco, the fool, smirks. He cranes his neck to look beyond us, and I can only imagine what he's hoping to see... or who.

"I wish I could say the same," Marco finally says.

"And why's that?"

"Because I was just notified that you've kidnapped one of my friends."

"Oh yeah, Alice is your friend?" Fender asks, taunting the man.

As Fender and Marco go back and forth in a verbal boxing match, Joker, Riker, Squirrel, and Piston slowly form a circle around our enemy and his men. Greaser and I stay near Fender, with the crate.

Marco swivels his head to take in my brothers. When he looks at Fender again, he's grinning.

"This won't end well for the Soulless Kings," he says.

"I beg to differ."

"What's the end game here? Take us out, and then what?"

"Don't know." Fender shrugs. "Sky's the fucking limit."

"I'll repeat myself... This isn't going to end well for you. There are people who will seek revenge for what happens here if you go through with what you have planned. Kill me, and they will come."

Our Prez, the man we all look to for guidance and direction, shakes his head and chuckles. But it doesn't last longer than split-second.

Royal

"Twatopatomus!" Fender shouts, surprising the hell out of us all.

I don't think he's ever used the code word... ever.

Something is definitely going on.

Greaser and I drop the crate, and it smashes open, spilling weapons onto the dirty concrete floor. Gunshots echo in the large space as everyone fires. I'd prefer a knife, but you never bring a knife to a gunfight. And one thing we knew about Marco, especially with the purchase he was trying to make, tonight was going to end one way and one way only... in a hail of bullets.

It takes less than three minutes for the shooting to stop, and Marco and his men are all lying in pools of blood.

"Anyone hurt?" Piston asks.

"Grazed arm," Joker says. "But nothing Gibson can't handle."

"Everyone else is good," Piston adds.

"How the fuck did he know, Prez?" Greaser demands.

"I don't kn—"

"Alice," I snap.

"If it was Alice, that means she got a phone somehow because we smashed hers."

"We gotta get back to the clubhouse," I shout as I turn and race toward the exit.

Fear sinks its talons into me like a vulture with roadkill. I don't wait for the others to follow. They will. There's no way in hell they're gonna stay back when they know there's a diabolical bitch within the same four walls as our women.

Our women?

Their women.

I tear out of the parking lot, gravel flying behind me as the tires gain purchase, and go as fast as the van allows. Two minutes later, the single headlights of six motorcycles close in on me. Fender and Piston pull around to lead the way, and we haul ass home.

The ride seems to take forever, with each passing mile bringing with it a new worry, a new nightmarish image to flash through my mind at what we'll find when we get there.

Logically, I know that my brothers and the women are safe. Alice is in the Nightmare Room, and it's impossible to break out. But she managed to tip off Marco, and that should be impossible from the Nightmare Room too.

There's a first time for everything.

Chapter Eighteen

I'm glad you're not dead.

Paige

"Maybe you should eat something."

I shake my glass, and the ice rattles against the glass. Parker frowns but takes it from me and fills it with more vodka and cranberry juice. When he sets it on the bar in front of me, I go to grab it, but it's snatched out of reach.

I spin on the stool at the owner of the offending hand and have to grab the edge of the bar to keep from toppling over. Not used to this much alcohol, I'm fairly certain I'm wasted.

"Oh, you're definitely wasted, hon," an older woman dressed in denim and leather says.

"What? How did... Who the fuck are you?"

The woman ignores my question and scowls at Parker. "Burly and I go away for a few weeks, and you forget about us, prospect?"

"Ah, no, no," he stammers.

Parker stammers... actually stammers. Who the hell is this bitch, and why is she scaring my prospect?

"For fuck's sake, who does she belong to?"

"I don't belong to anyone," I say with as much indignation as my drunk self can muster.

"Margo!" a voice I recognize shouts.

I twist again, and my vision blurs. Charlie's body, or at least I think it's her body, breezes past me as she throws herself at the bitch.

"Hon, it's Margo," the woman says. "My name is Margo, not bitch. I suggest you learn that before I have to beat it into you."

Wait... how does she know what I'm thinking? Fuck, did I say that out loud?

"Leave her alone, Mar," Charlie says with a laugh. "She's had a rough day."

"A rough day?!" I shriek. "You call what the psycho said a rough day?"

"Okay, will someone please tell me what is going on?" Margo demands. "I know we've been gone a while, but it seems like we've missed way too much."

"Hasn't Burly been checking in for updates?"

"Well, yeah, but I think Curly's been leavin' some shit out."

Charlie laughs. "Sounds about right. The man can take notes in church and keep this club's records in line, but when it comes to verbalizing information, he sucks ass."

"I don't belong to anyone," I repeat because it doesn't seem like they care about that particular fact.

"We heard you the first time," Margo says, but she doesn't sound as bitchy. "So, she a new Bangin' Betty or something?" she asks Charlie.

Royal

"Oh, shit, no." Charlie shakes her head and steps back to throw her arm around my shoulders. "This is Paige. She's, uh, well, I don't know exactly what she is. I'm guessing Royal's future ol' lady, but he hasn't claimed her yet."

"Claimed me? What are you tal—"

"He will," Margo says with conviction. "He's a good kid, and one of these days, he'll get his head outta his ass."

"Would you stop talking about me like I'm not here?"

"Nope."

I huff out a breath and turn back toward the bar. Parker is standing there with a grin on his face. I get the feeling he's trying not to laugh at my expense, but he might as well. No one else seems to care.

"You sure you're not hungry?" he asks me, his lips twitching.

"Pretty sure if I eat right now, it'll all come back up," I tell him. "I'm good."

"So, hon," Margo begins as she sits on the stool next to me. "Tell Mama Margo about this rough day you're havin'."

"Rough day," I repeat before snorting. "I didn't lose my keys or forget to take my multivitamin. Now *that's* a rough day."

"We really need to work on what defines 'rough' around here." Margo sighs. "Fine, not a rough day. What would you call it then?"

"Terrible, horrible, no-good..." My eyes widen. "Hey, that's part of a children's book title."

"This will get you nowhere," Charlie states. "C'mon, I'll show you why Paige here is drinking like a fish and making a horrible first impression."

Margo hops off her stool to follow Charlie, and I do the same. If they're going to see Alice, so am I.

When we reach the basement, Benny is sitting in the

folding chair in front of the Nightmare Room, and he eyes us suspiciously when he spots us.

"Uh, Charlie, what's going on?"

"Well, who the fuck are you?" Margo demands with her hands on her hips.

"Margo, meet Benny. One of the new prospects Royal recruited." Charlie grins. "Fucker's damn good at his job. Benny fits right in and doesn't bitch about the shit the guys put him through." She faces the prospect. "Benny, this is Margo. She's Burly's ol' lady. They've been on vacation, so you haven't met him yet, but you will."

"Burly will be here as soon as he's done unloading all our shit back at the house," Margo informs us. "

"It's nice to meet you," Benny says as he shakes Margo's hand.

"You too, prospect." She turns toward the monitor. "Who do we have here?"

"A stupid bitch," I mutter.

"Well, hon, she's in the Nightmare Room, so I figured that much. What's her name?"

"Alice. She was my best friend in the whole wide world." My tone resembles that of a petulant child, but no matter how hard I try, I can't change it.

Stupid alcohol.

"Paige and Alice grew up together," Charlie explains. "Long story short, Alice and her boyfriend claim to have seen some of the brothers killing two people, called the cops and got nowhere, and then talked Paige into helping to blackmail the club for money and to keep them alive."

Margo glares at me. "You agreed to it, didn't you?"

I throw my hands up. "Of course I did! She was my best friend. But she played me like a damn fiddle so I'm on the club's side now."

Royal

"I get it, Mar," Charlie begins. "Instinct is to hurt her. She could've created a world of trouble, but she ended up doing the right thing. And Royal's sweet on her, so we like Paige," she finishes with a grin.

"And she's a really good photographer," Benny adds.

Before he started his shift guarding the Nightmare Room, I was showing him some of the pictures on my phone. He gushed appropriately, and it felt good.

Not as good as when Royal told me my photographs are good, but still. It's nice to have others recognize my talent.

Royal... He has kind eyes.

"Good to know," Margo says as she faces the monitor, and her face hardens. "This the bitch who hurt you?"

I nod, not trusting myself to speak. Alice and I had it out last night, right there in that room, and it left me feeling empty. She tried to deny using my name, but I was way past furious and punched her in the face. That shocked her so much, she started talking.

And the things she said, the threats she made to the club, to me... I still have a hard time stomaching it.

"That black eye your handy work?" Margo asks.

I look at the screen, and again, simply nod.

"Nice job," she praises. "Next time, make the other eye match." Margo slaps Benny on the back. "Prospect, be a good little bitch and open the door for me."

Benny's eyes dart to Charlie, who only shrugs. "It's fine. Alice hasn't touched her food, and Margo just wants to make sure she's eating. We don't like our prisoners to suffer."

"Charlie, I don't know," Benny hedges. "Fender will have my ass if he finds out."

Charlie steps into the prospect's space and grabs him by his cut. "Then I guess he shouldn't find out, should he?"

Benny shakes his head. "No, ma'am."

"Dear fucking God," Charlie groans. "And you were doing so well too. The ma'am shit pisses me off, Benny. We've talked about this."

"Right. Okay."

Seeing Benny cower to these two women is... odd. I don't know him well at all, but he's seemed confident until now. Is he afraid of them, or Fender?

Benny opens the door and steps to the side so Margo can enter. Charlie and I follow her inside, and my stomach twists in knots when Alice glares at me.

"Come to attack me again," she snarls.

I don't even recognize her. Sure, she's physically the same person I've always known, but recognition isn't always just about what we can actually see. She's evil, right down to her soul, and I had no clue.

How the hell didn't I have a clue?

There were signs, tons of damn signs. But I ignored them all. I thought that made me a good person. Turns out, it only makes me a fool.

"I have nothing left to say to you," I tell her, hating the slight shake in my voice.

"Aw, poor Paige. She got played." Alice mock pouts, and I clench my fists. "I've got news for you, *friend*... I'm not done with you yet."

Charlie lunges at Alice, who's not tied to a chair, and grabs her by the hair to slam her head against the wall.

"Are you threatening her?" Charlie snarls.

Alice grins. "Nah. I'm just giving her a warning."

Charlie uses both hands to throw Alice to the floor, but it doesn't seem to faze her. She laughs maniacally, and it's yet another side to Al that I didn't know existed.

Is this what a psychopath is? I watch true crime shows

about them, and I always get frustrated with the friends and family of psychopaths who never realized who was in their life.

I get it now. I understand how that's possible.

The door to the Nightmare Room slams shut, causing Margo and I to spin around. Benny is standing there, with a gun pointed at Charlie. Adrenaline speeds through my veins and suddenly, I'm stone-cold sober.

I wish I weren't.

"Let her go," Benny snarls, the cowering idiot from earlier long gone. His confidence is back, only now it's ten times the amount he showed me before. "Don't make me pull this trigger."

"Wow," Margo says. "I love Royal, but fuck, he picked a bad one." She smirks at Benny. "And here I thought I was gonna like you."

Charlie straightens and steps away from Alice with her hands up. "Put the gun down, Benny."

"Not gonna happen," he says calmly and tilts his head. "Ya know, I almost felt bad for giving Alice my cell to tip off Marco. Everyone here has been far more welcoming than I expected. And let's face it, Alice is psycho. Bitch is fucking crazy."

"Shut up, Ben," Alice snaps as she gets to her feet and moves toward him.

"Right about now, I'm guessing your guys are bleeding out in that factory," Benny says as if he's talking about a leisurely Sunday drive. "I like them, so I'm gonna give you a chance to save their asses."

My heart stutters at the thought of Royal dying in a pool of his own blood. It cracks at the thought of a world without him in it.

What the actual fuck? That's gotta be the alcohol... right?

Charlie growls, and Margo backs up against the wall to slide down and sit on the floor.

What the fuck is she doing? Now is not the time to sit.

"Give us your phones, let us walk away without any fuss," Benny continues. "And I won't lock you in here. After five minutes, feel free to scramble to get to them."

"And if we don't let you go?" I ask.

"They'll all die," Alice answers matter-of-factly. "But know this... you kill us, Brock will come for you. And there will be no one left to protect you because Royal and Fender, and all those other apes will be dead."

"There's another option," Margo says casually.

Benny looks at her with a smirk. "Oh yeah? What's that?"

With the speed of someone half her age, Margo leans forward and grabs a gun out of a holster at her ankle. She aims for Benny and Alice, who have no time to react before she pulls the trigger, hitting them both between the eyes.

"Holy shit!" I exclaim.

"Well, that was fun," Margo says as she slides the gun back into its holster and stands. "What a welcome home party."

"Fender's gonna be pissed," Charlie comments as she crosses the room, stepping over the bodies like they're banana peels she doesn't want to slip on.

"He'll get over it," Margo says. "It's not like he'd expect you to sit back and let them get away."

"What is wrong with you two?!" I shout. "Fender's not going to be pissed. He's dead! And Royal's de—"

"You wanna tell her, or should I?" Margo asks Charlie.

"Tell me what?"

"Go ahead," Charlie says with a wave of her hand.

Royal

Margo walks toward me and rests her hands on my shoulders. "Fender isn't dead. And neither is Royal."

"But..." I dart my gaze to Alice and Benny before leveling it back on the crazy woman in front of me. "They said they were. They tipped Marco off."

"Yeah, I'm sure they did," Margo agrees patiently. "But if our boys were ready to be put six feet under, we'd know."

"No, you wouldn't," I insist. "How could you? They said—"

"She's right, Paige. We'd know." Charlie walks back to stand beside me. "Just... trust us. They're absolutely fine."

I shake my head, none of what they're saying makes sense. They're acting as if I'm the crazy one, but I'm not. They're not crazy either, but they are in denial. A deep, deep denial that will come back to bite them in the ass.

I open my mouth to try and reason with them, but before I can get a word out, the door to the Nightmare Room opens. The three of us slowly turn, and...

"What the fuck happened here," Fender snarls as he moves into the room to crouch next to the dead bitch and prospect.

"That's a funny story," Margo begins. "You see, it all started when Alice threatened Paige."

Royal rushes forward and grabs my hand. "She threatened you? Are you hurt? What did she say?"

"I'm fine," I snap. "I'm absolutely fine, but they're..." I swallow when I look at them again. My stomach rolls at the sight of all the blood. "They're not."

Fender straightens to his full height and narrows his eyes at his wife. "Charlie, we talked about this."

Margo's forehead wrinkles with confusion, but she says nothing. Royal doesn't even seem to notice that the air in the room has changed as he visually inspects me for injuries.

"We did," Charlie concedes. "If it helps, I didn't shoot them."

"You shouldn't have been in here in the first place," Fender shouts.

Charlie stiffens. "Just because I'm pregnant, you stupid oaf, doesn't mean I'm going to sit on the sidelines and not protect or defend our own. She threatened Paige, I reacted, they both threatened us all, Margo shot them. It's that simple."

"Wait," Royal says, whirling around to face them. "You're pregnant?"

Fender groans. "We agreed we weren't going to tell anyone until the second trimester."

"Shoulda thought about that before you started getting all growly and mean."

"Oh shit, that explains it," Royal says with a grin.

"Explains what?" I ask.

"Fender used the code word," he says.

"What?" I ask, confused as hell.

"You said twatopatomus?" Charlie asks excitedly.

"Thanks, asshole." Fender glares at Royal. "But yeah, that's why."

"I was wondering why you were acting weird. Glad to know it's nothing bad."

"Take your woman and get outta here," Fender barks. "Margo, I'm glad you and Burly are back, but next time, try for a less active return." He turns to Charlie. "As for you, I'm glad you're okay. But I swear to fucking hell, if you pull this kinda shit again, I'm gonna tan your ass."

"Promise?" Charlie bats her eyes at Fender.

"Woman," he snaps.

Royal

Royal grabs my hand. "We better go before things get ugly." He glances at the bodies. "Well, uglier."

He drags me out of the room and upstairs. Margo follows us, chattering on about how she should've known something was going on with Charlie because she wasn't drinking and Charlie always drinks, and yada, yada, yada.

When we reach Royal's room, he guides me to the bed and gently pushes me onto the mattress. He doesn't sit next to me, but instead crouches between my knees.

"You okay?"

"Yeah, I'm fine."

"You haven't said a word in a few minutes. And you're pale."

"I just watched two people get shot," I gripe. "One of whom was my best friend." I shake my head. "Ex best friend. How do people go from that to talk of pregnancy?"

Royal chuckles as he takes my hands and folds them in his. "Welcome to club life, sugar."

"I don't know how I feel about it," I admit.

"Well, you haven't run yet, so I'm hopeful."

I stare at him as if somehow, doing so will reveal everything I need to know about the man. Having loved Alice and doing whatever I could to protect her, only to be so horrifically betrayed... that changes things, changes everything.

I don't trust my judgment, not even a little. But something, some *unidentifiable thing*, is telling me to try.

"I'm glad you're not dead," I admit quietly.

"Yeah?"

"Benny said you were, and that scared me. So... yeah, I'm glad you're not dead."

"I am too, sugar."

Chapter Nineteen

I can win her over, I know I can.

Royal

One week later...

"How the fuck is this possible?"

I absently drum my fingers on the table as my brothers bitch and moan about the latest development in the Marco-Alice-Brock-Benny saga. Basically, there are no developments. We don't have shit. Squirrel has been diligently working to track down Brock, but he's gone underground, and we can't find him.

Harker hasn't been any help either. Apparently, he's been behind locked doors with higher-ups for days. He says he's trying to find out why Alice and Brock's arrest records were buried so deep, but I'm not sure I believe him.

I'm not sure I believe anything anymore.

My gut fucked me, then my head, then the world.

"Everyone has a footprint somewhere," Piston barks.

"Not Brock," Squirrel says. "I mean, there's a digital

footprint, but it stops the night everything went down with Marco, Alice, and Benny. And the other stuff like driver's license and last known address... we have them, but he's still nowhere to be found."

"This is bullshit!" I shout as I pound my fists on the table. "He's one person. It's not like he's got an army of men behind him. His cousin is dead, his girlfriend is dead, and he's a fucking nobody."

"He might be a nobody, but he was connected to a somebody," Fender says calmly, which only feeds my frustration. "Marco might be dead, but that doesn't mean his reach is."

"What am I supposed to tell Paige?" I ask.

Paige wanted to return to her loft almost immediately. Convincing her to stay this past week wasn't easy and talking her into taking the week off from work was even more difficult. Fortunately, Charlie and Margo had my back.

She likes them, and they like her, which works in my favor.

"Tell her the truth," Piston says. "I mean, don't give her more than you're permitted to, but you can be honest about the fact that we can't find Brock, and until we do, she's in danger."

"I don't think that's gonna matter to her," I admit. Shoving a hand through my hair, I heave a sigh. "She's not mine, so I have no sway over her decisions."

"So make her yours," Joker says.

"I don't..." I shake my head. These are my brothers, and I don't have to lie to them. Even if I'm lying to myself. "How? It's not like we met under the best circumstances. And I threatened to kill her. That tends to kill any prospect of a relationship."

"Brother, you're a Soulless King," Fender snaps. "Suck it up. None of us started our marriages off under good circumstances. Hell, Charlie was locked in the Nightmare Room too. And look at us now. Just fucking talk to her, tell her how you feel."

"That's just it," I counter. "I don't know how I feel."

"Seriously?" Piston smirks at me. "You call her 'sugar', you follow her around like a damn puppy, and you stare at her any time you think she's not looking. *And* you invited her to stay here with you, *in your room*, for a week. You know how you feel."

"But nothing's happened. I kissed her once just to shut her up, and I sleep on the goddamn floor."

"You've gotta be kidding me." Riker shakes his head. "Man, you are dumber than you look."

"Fuck off."

"You used to have game," Flash taunts.

"But she's not a game!"

"And that's your problem," Fender says. "You like her and have no clue what to do. But you don't have to do anything, Royal. Just be yourself. Talk to her, take her for a ride, get to know her. You're not a bad guy, and she knows it. She wouldn't be here otherwise."

"And if it's all one-sided?"

"Better to figure it out sooner rather than later," Gibson says magnanimously.

"Look at it this way," Trainwreck begins. "If she doesn't like you or whatever, you've got the Bangin' Betties to fall back on. And if you don't want them, you can always hire a hooker."

There was a time that might have appealed to me, but not now. Not since I met Paige.

Motherfucker.

Royal

I'm going to have to talk to her because I'm driving myself nuts over this. I'm going to have to forego free and easy for claimed and complicated.

But I don't have a choice. I didn't want to be in my head, to overthink things, but it's where I'm at so I might as well embrace it.

And if anyone could make me want to try, it's Paige. The way she smiles, the way she quietly thanks me every night for letting her have the bed, the way she lights up when anyone asks her about her work, the way she... is.

"Are we done here?" I ask, pushing my chair away from the table.

"We all know what you're gonna be doing the second I dismiss you," Fender teases. "And I will in a minute. First, can we all agree that we continue to hunt down Brock?"

Two thumps fill the room.

"And can we all agree that it would be in Paige's best interest to have one of us with her at all times until he's caught?"

"Fuck yes," I snarl as two more thumps are given.

"Okay. Dismissed."

I hurry out of the room, ignoring the taunting and chuckles behind me. When I left Paige for church earlier, she was still getting ready in my room, so I head straight for the stairs.

"Royal, what's going on?"

I skid to a stop and whirl around to see Paige sitting at the bar with Charlie. Neither are drinking, but they are staring at me like I'm a crazy person.

"Oh, um..." Nerves attack me from the inside out. "I was looking for you," I tell Paige.

"You were? Is everything okay? Is it Brock?"

The panic in her eyes levels me. I hate that in my hurry to have a conversation with her, I caused her to worry.

Charlie hops off the stool. "I'm gonna see if Fender's ready to go. We've got an OB appointment today, and I don't wanna be late."

From behind the bar, Margo smirks with a shake of her head. "She never was a good liar."

"She's lying?" Paige asks, now confused. "Why would she lie about going to the OB?"

"Oh, hon, she wasn't lying about that," Margo explains. "But that appointment isn't for another two hours. She's lying about why she was leaving. She saw the look on Royal's face and wanted to give you two some time alone."

"The look on his..." Paige turns to face me again. "Royal, what look is she talking about?"

I scramble to come up with an explanation, but the only thing that comes out of my mouth is, "Wanna go for a walk?"

"A walk?"

"I swear, Money Bags," Margo says with a chuckle. "I thought the guys taught you better than that. Take the poor girl up to your room and talk to her."

"Royal, do you need to talk to me? Is that what's going on?"

Oh. Dear. God. I'm fucking this up before I even get started.

"No. Yes." I groan. "Yeah, I do. Come upstairs with me?"

Paige shrugs. "Okay."

She crosses the room, and I rest my hand on her lower back to guide her up to my room. When I close the door behind us, my palms begin to sweat, and my head starts to spin.

Royal

"Are you okay?" Paige asks with concern. She grabs my arm and leads me to the bed, where she pushes me down to sit. "You look like you're gonna pass out."

"I think I might," I admit.

"Is it that bad?" She begins to pace. "I knew it. It is bad, isn't it? Something happened with Brock, right? Oh my God, the cops found out about Alice and Benny, didn't they? You're all in trouble. I can't believe this is hap—"

"I like you," I blurt and immediately snap my mouth closed.

She was spinning out, spiraling down a winding path of worst-case scenarios, and it was heart-breaking to watch. And sorta cute. But mostly heart-breaking because if I've learned one thing about Paige, it's that she feels everything very deeply.

Paige stops in her tracks and slowly spins to face me. "You... What?"

I stifle a groan and stand so I can be closer to her. Lifting her hand in mine, I repeat myself. "I like you, Paige. From the moment I heard your sultry voice, I was fucked. And then I made mistake after mistake, and here we are." I take a deep breath. "I like you, and here we are, forced together out of necessity, but I don't want it to be out of necessity."

Paige stares at me as if I've lost my mind. "You don't even know me."

"I know enough to know you're a woman worth my time. I know that you're stunningly beautiful." I brush a strand of hair behind her ear. "And you don't even know it. I know that you don't snore, but you do talk in your sleep, so softly that I have to strain to hear what you're saying. I know that you're fiercely loyal, even when it hurts you, and that when you love someone, you do it with your whole heart. I know your smile lights up a room, and you're insanely talented with a camera. I know you're sma—"

"Stop." Paige extricates her hand from mine and takes a step back. "Royal, those are not the words of a man confessing to like someone. Those are the words of a man who's pledging his life to someone. And..." She averts her eyes. "I'm not the girl for you."

"Why?"

She takes a deep breath before looking at me again. "Because I'm not the girl for anyone." The words are barely above a whisper. "Because men want girls like Alice, not me. Because... just because."

Fuck that!

"Look, I know I screwed up," I admit. "I saw you and freaked. You made me consider things I'd never thought about before. I've always been a one-night kinda guy. I won't lie about that. But, I don't know, I don't want that with you."

"Thanks," she scoffs.

"No, that's not what I meant." I take a step forward and grab her hand when she tries to step back again. "I want you, Paige. Make no mistake about that. I wanted you before I even saw you. But I also started to think about more, ya know? Because I didn't want to *just* fuck you. I wanted to get to know you, to spend time with you, and that's different for me. That's scary as hell."

"If you wanted me, why'd you choose Alice?"

"Because I'm an idiot. Because you scared me. Still do, if I'm being honest." I pull her closer to me, and shockingly, she doesn't resist. "Because I made a decision years ago to keep my life as easy and uncomplicated as possible, and Alice seemed to fit that bill."

"I'm not complicated," she grumbles.

Royal

"Yeah, sugar, you are. But I'm realizing that complicated isn't a bad thing if it's the right person. Complicated is just... more."

"I don't know what I'm supposed to do with this, how I'm supposed to react. You're not at all who I thought you were, but I don't know if that's enough, Royal."

"Do you like me?" I ask, trying to get somewhere, anywhere, with her.

"Yeah, I do. And that's..."

"Scary," I finish for her.

Paige sighs. "So damn scary. We live in two very different worlds."

"Opposites attract, right?"

She rolls her eyes. "Yeah, sure. But are we too opposite?"

"I don't know. But I want to find out."

"And all of this isn't just to get in my pants or to get me to stay here longer?"

Shit.

"To get in your pants, no," I tell her. "Although I wouldn't be opposed to that whenever you're ready. And it's not to get you to stay longer, but we do need to talk about that."

"No. Absolutely not. No, I can't stay."

"Can we finish one conversation before we have another?"

"Fine, we like each other. Conversation closed."

"Paige, don't do that. Don't hide behind your fear. You're stronger than that."

"I'm not hiding, Royal. I'm being realistic."

"So you won't even consider seeing if there's something between us? Is that what you're telling me?"

"No, that's not what I'm saying." She moves away from

me to sit on the bed. "Look, if I agree to *consider* seeing if there's anything between us, can we drop it? Please?"

That's not exactly what I was hoping for, but it'll have to do. I can win her over, I know I can. We've come a long way from where we started already, and more time can only help.

"Yes, we can drop it."

"Okay. I'll consider it."

I shift to stand in front of her. "You won't regret it, sugar. I promise."

"There's another conversation we need to have, and something tells me it's a doozy," she begins. "Don't make promises you can't keep. That definitely won't get you anywhere with me."

"Noted."

"Good."

"Now, about you staying..."

Chapter Twenty

Sleeping with Royal would only lead to sex with him, and that would lead to regret.

Paige

"Thank you for agreeing to this."

I drop my bag near the couch and stretch my arms over my head. Royal and I debated for two hours about whether or not I should stay at the clubhouse and ultimately, it was a debate I won.

"You didn't give me much choice," I remind him.

"But you got to come back to your loft."

"With what amounts to a bodyguard," I snap. "Treating me like I can't take care of myself is not how you win me over, ya know?"

"Look at it this way, with me here, there's more time for us to get to know each other better." Royal strides toward me after locking the door. "The faster we do that, the sooner you'll realize that you really do like me, and I'm worth your time."

I smack his chest playfully. "You're impossible."

We seem to have come to some sort of understanding. Or maybe it's just that I'm accepting that he's not going to give up unless or until I tell him definitively that he should. He's going to flirt, and I'm going to let him.

I might not like being babysat, but that doesn't mean I have to be miserable. Hell, maybe I'll even get to the point where I can be like him. One-night stands aren't my thing, but there's always exceptions.

No. He's not here for a fling. And you're not the fling type.

Tell that to my lady bits. I may have admitted to Royal that I like him, but I kept something back too. There was no way I was going to tell him that I want him as much as he wants me. Nope. Not happening.

Have a little fun, Paige. He's here, you're here... nothing wrong with sex between two consenting adults.

But there is something wrong with it if both parties don't share the same motivation. Royal likes me. He wants more with me. If I don't want that, how can I sleep with him knowing he'll get hurt?

Or you'll get hurt.

"Mind if I hop in the shower?" Royal asks, pulling me out of my head.

"No, of course not."

"Thanks." He starts toward the hallway. "Uh, bathroom?"

"Oh, right." I laugh nervously. "There's only the one... through my room."

"Hmmm."

I narrow my eyes at him. "What?"

"Nothing." He moves down the hall and out of sight. "I'll only be a few minutes," he calls right before he opens the door to my bedroom.

Royal

The pipes creak when he turns on the water, and I grab a bottle of water to cool off while I imagine him naked. Because he is naked... in my room... in my shower... he's naked.

And I want to see him.

It's your loft. Your bedroom. You can go in there if you want.

It wouldn't hurt to change into comfier clothes. As I step into my room, I can't help but wonder when I grew a pair. This isn't me. I'm not the woman who goes after a man for anything. I'm not... Alice.

And just like that, any thought of the naked man in my shower flees. I yank open my dresser drawer and pull out a pair of sweats and a t-shirt. And clean underwear for good measure.

I toss my dirty clothes in the direction of my hamper, and the water shuts off. The click of the shower door being released from the magnet as Royal opens it seems to echo off the exposed brick walls.

I rush to tug my clean panties over my hips and slip my arms into the shirt. I'm hurrying and hopping on one foot as I try to get my leg into my sweats. The bathroom door opens, and I whirl around so fast that I fall on my ass.

"Damn, sugar," Royal says as he lunges forward to offer me his hand. "Are you okay?"

No, I'm humiliated.

Heat spreads throughout my body, and when Royal helps me to stand, it only worsens because my skin grazes his. He's got a towel wrapped around his waist, water droplets rolling down his chest, and a happy little boner threatening to poke through the terry cloth barrier.

Happy? Definitely. Little? Not at all.

I groan, and he chuckles. "Here, let me help." Royal

bends to guide my leg into the sweatpants, and then slowly pulls the material up to my hips, his fingertips light as they tease my flesh. "There. Better?"

Incapable of speech, or coherent speech at least, I nod.

"You ready for bed?"

Bed? I don't think that's a good idea.

I nod.

Idiot!

"Okay. Will it bother you if I stay up for a while, maybe watch some TV?"

"N-no."

"Thanks. I usually do before going to bed but didn't want to back at the clubhouse since we only had the one room. But here I can go into the living room and watch, that way I won't disturb you."

"Okay."

Royal strides back into the bathroom and when he returns, he's wearing his usual basketball shorts and t-shirt. Now that he's covered, breathing becomes easier.

"What time do you have to be at the studio tomorrow?" he asks before stepping out of the bedroom.

"I like to be there by eight," I tell him. "Evelyn will probably get there before me though so if I'm a few minutes late, it's no big deal."

"Evelyn's your assistant, right?"

My insides beam at the fact that he remembered. "Yep."

"And George is the other photographer?"

"Uh huh."

"Got it. Well, I'll set an alarm on my phone so I'm up in time. See ya in the morning."

"Royal!" I yell as his footsteps thud on the floor in the hallway. I race to the doorway and lean my head around to look at him.

Royal

"Yeah?"

"Um..." I take a deep breath. "That couch isn't that comfortable to sleep on so... If you want to sleep in here, you can." His eyes widen ever so slightly. "I mean, in the bed, not on the floor. You've slept on the floor for a week and..." I shake my head. "You can sleep in here if you want."

Embarrassed, I turn around and lean against the wall where he can't see me.

"Night, Paige," he calls.

"Night."

Sunlight streams through the one window in my bedroom, and I squint against it before rolling over to shut off my alarm. The bed is empty, and while it's disappointing, it's probably for the best. Sleeping with Royal would only lead to sex with him, and that would lead to regret.

Thinking clearly is easier in the light of day.

And I really don't want to regret anything with him. I do like him. Once I accepted that George was right about good people doing bad things, it was easy to like him.

Does he scare me? A little, at times. But I trust that he won't hurt me. I don't know why. Probably because he's had every opportunity and instead of pain, he's brought comfort. He's as gentle as he is hard, and I find I very much like the dichotomy.

"Morning."

I glance around the room and don't see him, so I scoot to the edge of the bed and glance down. Royal is lying on his back, a throw pillow under his head and a small blanket covering him from the waist down.

"Hi."

"I was hoping you were gonna shut that damn thing off. Woman, you've gotta change that sound. It is not a good sound to wake up to."

"What?"

"Your alarm," he clarifies. "It's a fucking car horn!"

I grin. "I know. It's the only thing that gets me up in the morning. Otherwise, I'd sleep right through it."

"I know much better ways to wake you up."

I reach behind me and grab one of my pillows, and then throw it at him.

"Hey, what was that for?"

"Impossible."

I toss my blankets off of me and climb out of bed to trudge to the bathroom so I can shower and get ready for work. A knock on the door startles me, and I jump. Thank God he can't see me.

"You want coffee or something to eat?" he asks through the barrier.

"Sure."

As soon as his footsteps disappear, I breathe a sigh of relief. It doesn't take me long to get showered and dressed. I opt to pull my hair into a messy ponytail since we don't have any photo sessions on the schedule today, and I forego all makeup. I don't like the stuff unless it's a special occasion, and a Monday at work is not that.

You wore makeup when you went to talk to Royal about Alice.

"Shut up," I mumble.

"Who are you talking to?"

I whirl around and see Royal standing in the doorway to my bedroom, fully dressed and looking way too sexy for my liking.

"No one."

"As long as you're not getting answers, there's no shame in talking to yourself."

"I wasn't talking to myself."

Royal shrugs. "Okay. Whatever you say."

I push past him and walk out to the living room. The smell of coffee permeates the air, so I divert to the kitchen to pour myself a cup. After drinking half of the liquid caffeine, I feel more energized and ready to face the day.

"I talked to Fender while you were in the shower," Royal says. "Still nothing on Brock. But we won't stop until we find him."

"I know." I grab my purse off the counter. "We better go."

He looks at me funny, like he wants to say something but doesn't know how I'll react. But he says nothing as we head out to my car. He says nothing the entire drive to the studio. And he says nothing beyond 'hey' and 'what's up' when I introduce him to Evelyn and George.

The morning goes by quickly because I have a lot of work to catch up on. Royal brought a laptop with him, so he spends his time doing, well, whatever it is he does, and it isn't until almost noon when he finally speaks.

"Why don't you take a break?"

I look up from the email I'm typing. "Not yet. I've got a few more things to finish first."

"You know the work will still be here after, right?"

"Yeah, I do. But I was gone for a week. While everyone has been great about me being *sick*, that doesn't mean the work doesn't pile up."

"Okay, boss," he says with a grin.

I finish the email, and just as I hit send, my cell phone rings. I let it go to voicemail because I don't want to get stuck in a conversation. But when the device pings with the voicemail notification, I hit play to listen to it on speaker phone and lean back in my chair.

"You killed my cousin and my girlfriend."

I lunge forward at the same time Royal does, both of us grabbing at the phone. We stare at each other as Brock's voice sends terror through me.

"You can hide behind the club as long as you want, bitch, but I'm coming for you. You'll never be safe."

The call ends, and I fall back into my chair. Royal takes his own cell out of his cut and within seconds he's talking to Fender, asking him to get Squirrel to trace the call. I tune him out and rub my temples to stop my head from throbbing apart.

After Royal is done on his call, he walks around my desk and pulls me up into his arms. Neither of us says anything for a few minutes, but the silence becomes deafening beyond comprehension.

I lean back to look him in the eyes.

"I think I'm ready for that break now."

Chapter Twenty-One

It might no longer be my thing, but it's her thing. And she's my thing.

Royal

"How's she holding up?"

I switch the phone to my other ear and glance at Paige to make sure she's not listening in. When I'm sure she's occupied with the couple she's photographing, I return my attention to Trainwreck.

"Not well," I admit. "She's staying busy, but I worry that she's overdoing it."

"If it's how she deals, then it's a good thing."

"Not if it's draining the life out of her," I snap. "She barely eats, barely sleeps. And when she does sleep, she has nightmares. I hold her through them, but I don't know if it helps."

After that first night, Paige insisted that I sleep in the bed with her, but nothing ever happens. Not for lack of wanting though. I want her, so fucking bad. And if the way her nipples pebble against my chest in sleep is any indication, the feeling is mutual. But I haven't made a move.

I want her to know that my feelings for her aren't based on my cock. I need her to know that. If we have a shot in hell of working, that's important. And I'll continue to take cold showers until I'm sure she knows.

"I'm sorry, man," Trainwreck commiserates. "We're all working like hell to find the bastard."

"I know you are. And I appreciate it. So does she."

"Any more voicemails?"

My blood boils as I replay the message from Brock in my mind. "No, just the one."

"That's good."

"Yeah, I guess. I kinda wish he'd make a move because this waiting, this not knowing...

it's driving us both mad."

"Look, I think you both just need something that's not work or club related. Take her on a date or something," he suggests. "What does she like?"

"Seriously? You have to ask?"

"Photographs." He chuckles. "Right. Well, take her to an art gallery or some shit. One that features actual pictures. She'll eat that up."

"Not a bad idea. Any clue where one of those places is?"

I know where there are plenty back where I grew up, but here, in Oregon, it's not my scene.

"Dude, you know how to Google shit, so Google it."

"Fuck off."

"Hey, I gotta run. Flash and I are gonna go check out another address Squirrel wants us to run down. I'll let you know if it's anything."

"Thanks, brother."

Royal

"Anytime."

I disconnect the call and lean against the wall to watch Paige work. She's smiling and laughing with her clients, but it doesn't reach her eyes. I don't know if an art gallery will do the trick if her work doesn't. She loves her work. Hell, she fucking *lives* for it. But I'll try anything.

"Something is going on with her."

I glance to my left to see Evelyn standing a few feet away, a concerned look on her face as she watches Paige.

"She's got a lot on her plate right now, that's all."

I know she and Paige are friends, but Paige made it clear she doesn't want Evelyn or George to know all the details about Alice, so she's basically told them nothing.

"Royal, you seem like a nice enough guy, but Paige is fragile. She won't say it, and I know you won't, but I know something happened between her and Alice."

I stifle my groan. "What makes you think that?"

"Because Alice used to call the studio or Paige's cell phone daily. Like multiple times a day, to the point of distraction. And she hasn't called in over two weeks. Something happened, and Paige is hurting, and I just want to help. How can I help?"

"I wish I knew," I admit. "But I promise, I'm taking care of her. The best I know how anyway."

"Good. Because whatever happened with Alice has cracked Paige wide open. And if you split her in two, if you break her completely, I'll make your life a living hell."

With those parting words, Evelyn walks toward Paige to help her finish out the session. I like Evelyn. She's loyal, and she loves Paige. Those are two things I understand wholeheartedly.

Love?

Ten minutes later, the clients leave, and Paige flops

down in one of the chairs along the wall near where she was taking the pictures. I make my way to her and sit down.

"Do you have a lot of work left to do before you can go for the day?"

"Yeah." She yawns.

"And it can all wait," Evelyn says when she sits on the other side of Paige. "Or I can do it."

"No, no, I'm good," Paige insists.

"You're dead on your feet, sugar," I say. "Why don't you let Evelyn finish up? I'll drive you home so you can take a hot bath and just relax the rest of the night."

"That sounds heavenly."

"Then what's holding you back?"

Paige slaps her hands on her thighs and stands. "Too much to do."

She starts to walk away from me, but I'm done. I can't watch her do this anymore. I scoop her up and toss her over my shoulder.

"Evelyn, if you need her, wait until morning," I call out as I carry Paige down the hall to the back door of the studio.

"I won't need her," Evelyn shouts in reply.

"What are you doing?" Paige demands when we step outside. "I've got wo—"

I smack her ass, and she grunts.

"What was that for?"

"Kissing you to shut you up wasn't happening with you up there," I begin. "So I spanked you instead."

"I don't like being spanked," she pouts.

"Duly noted. I'll keep that in mind."

When we reach her car, I set her on her feet, and she sways slightly. I steady her with my hands on her shoulders.

"Dammit, you need to stop killing yourself," I snap.

"I'm not."

"You are. You're about to pass out, yet I'm guessing you're having an internal debate about whether or not you can outrun me to go back inside and work some more."

I arch a brow and wait for her reply. Paige crosses her arms over her chest, and I swear she's about to stomp her foot, but she catches herself.

"I'm fine."

"You're not fine." I reach around her to open the door. "Get in the damn car."

She stares at me for a moment, her eyes silently demanding me to back off, but I've got news for her. I'm not backing off. Not now, and probably not ever.

Finally, she huffs out a breath and gets in the passenger seat. I slam the door and stalk around the hood of the car, joining her on the driver's side.

"And don't even think that you're coming to work tomorrow," I bark as I start the engine.

"But I ha—"

"You don't have anything." When she narrows her eyes at me, I smirk. "You shared your schedule with me, remember? So, no, Paige, you don't have to work tomorrow. But what you do have to do is have some fun."

"How am I supposed to have fun when that lunatic is out there somewhere?" she snaps.

"That's where I come in."

"And what the hell is that supposed to mean?"

"It means, sugar, that I'm taking you out on a date."

* * *

"Why won't you tell me where we're going?"

Paige has asked me at least a dozen times since

yesterday where I was taking her. And every time, I refuse to tell her.

"Just make sure you're wearing jeans and your boots."

"Yeah, got it," she huffs as she stands from the couch to go take a shower.

I found a photography museum in the city that I'm taking her to, and then after, we're going to dinner. Nothing fancy, but it's not work or club business or Brock, so I think she'll enjoy it.

I hope she enjoys it.

While she gets ready, so do I. I'm not wearing anything special, just jeans and a Henley, but I do spray on a little cologne and put gel in my hair. I haven't been on an actual date in years, so I don't know if I'm doing this right, but oh well. It is what it is at this point.

"Does this work?"

I turn from the island where I was scrolling through my phone while waiting for her, and my breath hitches. My mouth dries out, and my pulse races as I take in her outfit. She definitely put more thought into it than I did.

Dark wash jeans hug her curves, and the strategically placed tears in the thighs expose just enough skin to tempt a saint. She's wearing a black and orange flannel that I haven't seen before, and underneath is a black tank with lace trim that teases her cleavage. The tank doesn't touch the denim, and I have to remind myself that today isn't about sex as I take in the sliver of visible stomach.

On her feet are the same boots she wore that first night I saw her, and her hair is in loose waves that frame her face. And that face... holy fuck, that face. It's perfect with a hint of blush, lip gloss, and eye shadow.

She's perfect.

"You look incredible," I tell her. "You look... irresistible."

Paige's cheeks flush a deeper shade of pink than her blush, and I smile knowing I have that effect on her.

"You look nice too," she says shyly.

"Thanks, sugar."

I close the distance between us, my boots thudding against the floor in time with my heartbeat. Cupping her cheek, I urge her closer as I lower my lips to hers. Paige's hands slide up my chest, and for a moment I fear she's going to push me away, but instead she fists my shirt and moans.

Today isn't supposed to be about sex, but fuck if I don't want to make it about exactly that. I swallow the breathy moans, the sensual sighs that escape her mouth, and glide my tongue across her lips. Tentatively, so as not to come across as pushy, I dart my tongue to tangle with hers, and she doesn't hesitate.

Yes!

My cock hardens beneath my jeans, and it becomes almost unbearable when Paige presses her body against mine. I kiss her for a moment longer, but then I have to stop. I have to... before I'm not able to.

She whimpers when I break the kiss, and it's a full ten seconds before she opens her eyes to look up at me. Her lips are swollen, and her pupils are dilated.

"I..." She clears her throat. "I want you, Royal."

"Feeling's mutual," I say honestly. "But first, I'm taking you on this date."

"Okay."

We take Tyche to the gallery, and despite being nervous, Paige adapts to riding on the back of my bike like a pro. Having her behind me, though, is some form of sweet torture. It takes me ten miles before I work up the guts to hold onto her thigh, but once I do, it hits me that riding never felt so good.

When I park in the parking garage across the street, I don't want to get off the Harley, and Paige even hesitates. But eventually, we both snap out of our motorcycle induced stupor.

"I can't believe you brought me to an art gallery," she comments as we cross the street to the entrance.

"Why not?"

"You're a biker. Just didn't think this would be your kinda thing."

I'm rich, educated, and have spent hours upon hours in art galleries and museums. Sure, it might no longer be my thing, but it's her thing.

And she's my thing.

"Don't judge a book by its cover, Paige. You're likely to miss all sorts of things that way."

We spend hours walking through the large rooms that are filled with photographs. The current exhibit features local photographers, and as we near the end, I can't help but wonder why none of her pictures are here. When we get to the restaurant for dinner, I ask her as much.

"I don't know." She shrugs. "I love what I do, but I don't want to share all of it with the world, ya know? Some of it, the stuff I'm really passionate about, I do for me or my clients, not for people who know next to nothing about true art to pick it apart because they don't like the lighting or whatever."

"Makes sense."

"Who knows? Maybe someday I'll want my pictures on display in galleries, but for now, I'm happy with Castor Photography Studios." Her words are positive, but her expression isn't.

"If you're so happy, why do you look sad when you talk about it?"

"It's just... everything with Alice screwed it all up for me." She huffs out a humorless chuckle. "I never told you this, but Alice bought me the studio. Well, loaned me the money anyway. I worked there for Stuart Castor, the original owner, all through high school. And when he retired, he offered it to me for a really good deal. I was broke back then so she gave me what I needed. I paid her back, of course. I do well with my business. More than well," she adds, but there's no bragging in her tone. Just fact. "I guess it's hard to find the joy in a dream a psychopath paid for."

"She may have loaned you the money, but you built the dream."

"Yeah, I guess."

"No, Paige, no guessing. I've watched you work for a while now, and I know part of your drive is the need to forget about everything else that's going on, but it's also because you simply don't quit. Even at the darkest moments of your life, you're prioritizing your clients, the studio. You built your success, and you should be proud of that." I lean back in my chair. "I know I'm proud of you."

"You are?"

"Of course, I am. You're the perfect woman. Smart, beautiful, hard-working, loyal, and all the other incredible qualities you possess."

"I'm not perfect."

"You don't get it," I say, the barest hint of heat in my tone. "You are, Paige. You're perfect for me."

Paige shifts in her chair. "I'm starting to feel the same about you."

I can't stop the grin that spreads. "Yeah?"

"Yeah."

"Hey, whaddya say we order dessert to go and ge—"

"Sir, I'm so sorry to interrupt," the waitress says as she

leans close so as not to be overheard. "But a gentleman just came in and asked me to give you this."

She hands me a folded piece of paper. I take it and glance around the restaurant to see if I recognize anyone.

"What gentleman?" I ask when she straightens.

"He left, sir," she says apologetically. "I asked him for a name, but he refused to give one. He said that you'd know who it's from. I really am sorry."

"It's okay. Thank you."

Once she's gone, I focus on Paige for a moment because I know, deep in my gut, that as soon as I unfold this piece of paper, the night is over.

"Royal?" Paige prods.

Taking a deep breath, I open the note, and my entire body goes numb at the words.

ENJOY THE DATE. IT'LL BE YOUR LAST WITH HER.
-B-

"We need to leave," I bark and shove away from the table. "Right now, Paige."

Paige's eyes widen, but she doesn't argue. She stands, and I toss a wad of cash on the table to cover the bill. Grabbing her hand, I lead her through the dining area, and out the front door, but I guide her down the sidewalk, in the opposite direction of Tyche.

"Where are we going?" she asks, fear heavy in her tone.

"To the clubhouse," I tell her. "But I have to make a call first."

We reach the end of the block, and I push her against the wall so I can shield her from any danger that approaches. I grab my cell from my back pocket and call Fender. He answers on the fourth ring.

Royal

"Aren't yo—"

"I've got a problem, Prez," I snap.

"What's up?"

"Brock's following us," I spit out. Paige trembles against me, and I hate that I'm scaring her, but I don't have a choice. "I'm gonna take the scenic route to my bike and then burn rubber to the clubhouse."

"Royal, stay there. I'll send some brothers to get you home."

"No, Prez." I glance around, but I don't see Brock anywhere. But I feel him, his eyes. It's like a thousand needles are pricking my spine. He's here, but he's hiding. "We're sitting ducks here. I can outrun him on Tyche. We'll be safer that way. Just make sure the gate's open because we'll be coming in hot."

"Man, I don't like this."

"I don't fucking like it either," I bark, no longer trying to be quiet. "But I'm not gonna sit here and wait for him to do something. I wouldn't be a Soulless King if I did."

"Fine. But I'm sending Piston and Greaser so they can at least meet up with you along the route home and give backup if needed."

"I'll share my location in case I have to detour. Later, Prez."

I disconnect the call and put my phone back in my pocket.

"Paige, I'm gonna need you to do exactly as I say, okay?" She nods, and we start walking. "Good. We're gonna walk around the block to get to my bike. We need to move fast, so climb on and hold on tight. No matter what happens, do not scream and startle me. Hold on tight, no screaming," I repeat.

"I'm scared."

"I know, sugar. But I'm not going to let a damn thing happen to you, okay?"

"Royal, is he really here? Did Brock really follow us?"

"Yeah, he did. And believe me when I say, he's going to regret that he did."

Paige squeezes my hand as we turn the last corner and see Tyche only a few feet away. As I help her onto the Harley, I take in our surroundings. That pin prick feeling of being watched has faded, but I don't trust it.

I get her settled on the bike and straddle the seat in front of her. She wraps her arms around my waist, and I rev the engine before tearing away from the curb. I weave through the minimal traffic, and as soon as I hit the highway, I open her up.

It doesn't take long for me to relax away from the city as it's easier to spot a tail. And I haven't clocked one for the last six miles. I ease my grip on the handlebars and shift my hand to Paige's thigh. As soon I connect, she presses her cheek to my back, letting me know in her own way that she's okay.

We're only on the highway for fifteen miles, and I slow to take the exit toward the clubhouse. As I turn right and start to speed up, headlights flash from the side of the road. For a split-second, I think it's an unmarked cop car, but then the light barrels straight for us.

"Hold on!" I shout to be heard over the engine, and Paige stiffens.

I swerve in time to avoid being struck by the car, but I can't react fast enough to correct my steering, and I'm forced to lay the bike down in order to dodge the semi-truck in the opposite lane.

A horn blares, drowning out the crush of metal. When I stop sliding across pavement, every inch of me screams in

Royal

pain, but adrenaline courses through my system. I roll to my side and see Paige lying, unmoving, about five feet away.

"P-Paige," I call out, my voice shaking.

Brakes squeal, and I turn toward the sound thinking it's help, or even my brothers, and collapse onto the ground.

"Help's here, Paige. Hold on. Just—"

Blinding agony rips through my skull, and my vision blurs.

"Oh yeah, help's here all right."

Brock?

I try to fight him off as he drags me toward Paige, but I'm too weak.

"Paige, wake u—"

Brock kicks me in the face, and everything goes black.

Chapter Twenty-Two

Fuck you, Alice. I got the guy.

Paige

"Wakey, wakey."

With a groan, I try to lift my arm, but it only moves a few inches before cold metal digs into my wrist. My eyes fly open, and panic wells in my chest as I take in the concrete walls surrounding me. The space reminds me of the Nightmare Room, but there are enough differences that I know that's not where I am.

"Wh-where's Royal?" I croak.

Brock strides across the wood plank floor and crouches next to the cot he has me chained to.

"He didn't make it."

"No, no, no." I shake my head, uncaring that the room spins when I do or that my neck feels like it'll snap with the movement. "I heard him. He was talking to me. He can't—"

Brock's face contorts with rage after he backhands me

across the face, splitting my cheek open with the ring he's wearing. Blood trickles from the wound, and if it didn't hurt so bad, it would tickle with how slow it traces a path to my chin.

"Were you that upset when Alice died?" he sneers.

"He was talking to me," I repeat. "He's not dead. I don't believe you."

"Well, fortunately for me, what happens here doesn't hinge on you believing me."

Brock grips the edge of the blanket I hadn't noticed was covering me, and as he straightens, he slowly eases it from my body. The material is rough, like wool, and it scrapes my already irritated skin. Cool air rushes over my flesh, causing goosebumps to pop up, and I shiver.

He slides his eyes from my face to my chest, and down to the apex of my thighs. The blanket is dropped to the floor, and he unbuttons his jeans before shoving them down and grabbing his dick as his gaze touches every inch of me.

I turn my head away, unable to bear the sight of him jacking off.

"Look at me," he demands.

"No."

"Fucking look at me!"

I roll my neck, but keep my eyes squeezed shut.

"Paige, open them." His voice is jerky, and I can only assume it's from the rapid movement of his hand.

"No."

There's a pause in his heavy breathing and then a distinctive click.

"Unless you want a bullet in your brain, open your fucking eyes!"

My lids are heavy, but I force them open. Bile rises up

my throat, and when he grunts out his release, vomit spews from my mouth.

Brock only laughs. "Alice wasn't a watcher either," he comments dryly and pulls his pants back up with one hand, the gun still in the other. "She preferred to be an active participant."

I continue to heave up the dinner I had with Royal until my stomach is empty. Sweat breaks out on my skin, which makes me shiver even more. I spit as much as I can to clear the taste from my mouth, and when there's no saliva left, I twist to wipe my lips on the dirty mattress.

"Damn, Paige. You kiss your biker with that mouth?"

"Where is he?"

"I told you, he's dead."

My memory flashes, and my pulse skitters.

"But if our boys were ready to be put six feet under, we'd know."

"She's right, Paige. We'd know. Just... trust us. They're absolutely fine."

"Where the fuck is he, Brock?" I ask again. "And don't tell me he's dead."

"Okay," he says conversationally. "He's not dead."

Relief crashes over me, and I sag into the mattress. But it's short-lived when he speaks again.

"Royal is unalive. He's pre-zombie. He's no longer breathing, his heart stopped, the blood in his veins no longer flows, his existence came to an abrupt end." He walks to the door and turns the lock before pulling it open. "No matter how I say it, the reality remains the same. He's gone. And you're here... with me."

With those parting words, he's gone, and the snick of the lock engaging seems to echo around me.

Royal

We'd know.
We'd know.
We'd know.
Royal isn't dead. He can't be.
I'd fucking know.
Wouldn't I?

When Margo and Charlie spoke about knowing if their men were dead, they were speaking from a place of love, of devotion, of being so in tune with another human that no matter the distance, they would know, with certainty, if something was wrong.

And after spending time with the Soulless Kings and their ol' ladies, after witnessing the bond they all have, I believe them.

But they love their men. And I...

He's not dead. I'd know.

I think I fell a little bit in love with Royal when he asked me about the picture of Darla on my phone. He may have been a complete and total asswipe that night, but he cared enough about my feelings to ask about something he deemed important to me.

It's been weird with him since then. Certainly a lot of highs and lows, twists and turns. But since he's been staying at my loft, it's like he's a different person. And maybe he's not different at all. Maybe he's just finally being the real him.

So, yeah, I love him. The good, the bad, and the ugly. Because to love someone is to accept them for exactly who they are.

And if the panic I experienced, the utter devastation that Brock saying Royal is dead caused is any indication, not only do I love the man, but he's it for me.

Fuck you, Alice. I got the guy.

Shaking the ridiculous thought from my mind, I focus on the knowledge that Royal isn't dead—because he isn't, dammit—and try to figure out a way to get the fuck out of this hellhole.

Chapter Twenty-Three

I'm sorry, Paige. I'm so fucking sorry.

Royal

"Where's Paige?"

Brock tsks and shakes his head. "Oh, don't you worry about that cunt." He grabs his crotch and smirks. "I've taken real good care of her."

I lunge, but the chain around my wrist yanks me back until I slam into the concrete wall. My brain rattles around in my skull, but I push past the pain and hang on to the fury.

"I swear to fuck, you're a dead man," I snarl. "You hear me? Dead!"

"Yet, you're the one chained to a wall."

"What do you want from us?" I demand.

I have no idea how long I've been in this room, but the moment I regained consciousness, I saw my surroundings for what they were: a piss-poor attempt at a Nightmare Room replication.

Too bad it's not accurate. I could use the hidden weapons the real deal has.

"Nothing much, really," Brock says. "You killed my cousin. So there's revenge for that. And then you killed the love of my life. So revenge for that." He nods as if satisfied with his answer. "Yeah, I think that's fair. Two lives for two lives."

"No one raped Alice," I sneer, disgusted by the image of him forcing himself on Paige that plagues my mind.

"Their loss. Alice is—was—dynamite in the sack."

"Where is Paige?" I ask again.

"Does it matter? It's not like you could get to her even if I told you."

"You won't get away with this. The Soulless Kings will find us, and they'll kill you."

"And how are they gonna do that? I smashed your phone at the scene of the crash. Paige's too."

"You think they need GPS locations to find us?"

"Yeah, I'm not worried. None of you even came close to finding me before."

"You're a de—"

"A dead man," he snaps. "Yeah, yeah, so you tell me. But ya know what?"

"What?"

Brock walks toward me, pulling something from behind his back as he does. When he reaches me, he ties a rope around my neck in a slipknot. Fear slithers through me, but I refuse to show it.

"I'm tired of listening to you talk," he says. "It's my turn."

"If you're gonna strangle me, then strangle me. I'm not interested in what you have to say."

He pulls the knot tight, cutting off my airway. I try to

reach for the cord, but my hands won't reach with the chains. Black spots dance before me as I struggle to breathe, and just before I pass out, he loosens the rope.

I suck in lungfuls of oxygen, and when my vision clears, I lift my head to glare at him.

"That was fun," I taunt.

"When I met Alice, I knew she was perfect for me." Brock keeps the rope in his hand, but he starts to pace the length of the room. "It was my cousin who pushed me to talk to her. Marco was always after chicks, but even he let Alice go for me. I'd come to Oregon with Marco a few years ago to scope the place out, see if he could make his operations work here. We went out to the bar one night, and there she was."

Each pass of the room stretches the rope to its maximum length, and until Brock turns on his heel to pace in the other direction, I lose the ability to breathe. But I don't struggle. I don't yell or beg or make any noise whatsoever. Because as long as he keeps walking, I know I won't die.

He just has to keep walking and talking.

"Was she always crazy, or did you make her that way?"

"Oh, Alice was always psycho." He laughs. "Literally, man. She was a psychopath. And for some reason, she liked me. Well, as much as she was capable of liking anyone. Marco recognized what she was pretty early on, so he invited us on vacation and gave us a proposition."

"To work for him?"

"How'd you know?" He stops in front of me and tilts his head with curiosity.

"Does it matter?" I counter.

"No, I guess not." Brock starts to pace again. "Anyway, if we agreed to work for him when he needed us, he'd pay for us to travel. We didn't need his money, but it still seemed like it would be fun, so we agreed."

"How did Alice do that without Paige getting suspicious?"

"The trips were always quick. A few days here, a weekend there." Brock shrugs. "Paige was always so wrapped up in that stupid studio, she barely had time for Alice. A studio Alice paid for, by the way."

"And was paid back," I say, infuriated on Paige's behalf.

"That's neither here nor there." He flicks his wrist dismissively. "Now where was I? Oh, yes. Travel."

"Is there a point to story time, or is your plan to bore me to death?"

Brock yanks on the rope, holding it tight for almost a full minute. When he releases it, he stalks toward me and grabs a fistful of my hair.

"I really want you to understand why you're dying," he tells me, and without more than a second's pause, he continues. "When Alice and I saw you and the others killing those men in that alley, Alice came up with the brilliant idea to blackmail you. Again, she didn't need the money. It was all about the thrill for her. So she called the cops, pretended to be Paige, and then we went to Paige's loft the next night and poured out the whole sob story."

"And where does Marco factor into this?"

"Other than encouraging us to do it... nowhere. He's my cousin, and it was a stroke of luck, or extreme misfortune depending on how you look at it, that he was wheeling and dealing with the Soulless Kings at the same time."

"Jesus," I mutter.

"Paige was doing so well too. She even followed you to that first meeting with Marco." He grins. "I gotta hand it to her, I did not see that coming." Pride is threaded in his tone. "But then she grew a conscience."

"And when she found proof that it wasn't her on the call, your plan was fucked."

"Alice's plan!" he shouts. "It was her plan."

"Okay."

"But yes. Paige fucked it all up."

"And where does Benny fit in?" I ask, genuinely curious. The thought that I recruited him doesn't sit well with me. Fender and the guys don't blame me, but I can't shake the idea that I failed them. "He was recruited before that night in the alley."

"Another stroke of luck, you could say. He was already working for Marco. Had been since he was in his teens. When Marco decided he wanted to pursue a deal with the Soulless Kings, he had Benny show up at that open house party. I knew nothing about him before we called Marco with our plan to blackmail the club."

Fucking hell, this all happened because of a sequence of coincidences. One event rolled into another into another, like a snowball rolling down a hill, only to culminate in the death and mayhem version of the abominable snowman.

"Anyway, you know the rest," Brock says. "Paige ratted, the club killed Marco and then Alice, and now I'm killing you and Paige."

Keep him talking. This can't be the end. If he talks, I live... Paige lives.

"I do have one question for you," I say.

"Just one?" I nod. "Okay, shoot."

"Other than your relation to Marco, I'm not sure what purpose you served in all of it. I mean, Marco still would have met Alice in that bar, she still would have witnessed my crime, and the whole plan still goes down."

Brock's face hardens as it turns a deep shade of angry red. He yanks the rope, but this time, he doesn't let go. And grabs the rope, inch by inch, as he stalks closer, and when he's standing a few inches away, he pulls a knife from his pocket.

Missed that.

I jerk against the chains, but it doesn't do me any good. I'm trapped.

"None of it would have happened without me," he snarls, his hot breath wafting across my face. "None of it."

The black dots appear, and the darkness begins to tug on me, to lure me into its depths.

"None of it," he snarls.

He plunges the knife into my stomach. Once, twice, three times he stabs me. "Poetic isn't it?" he taunts. "You strangle and stab and now you're being strangled and stabbed."

He thrusts the blade into my side as he twists the rope around his fist. I want to struggle, but I don't. There's no point. I'm a dead man.

Only one thought remains as darkness sucks me from this world...

I'm sorry, Paige. I'm so fucking sorry.

Chapter Twenty-Four

I think I'm in love with you.

Paige

Waiting is bullshit. I hate waiting.

I have no idea how long Brock has been gone, but if I had to guess, I'd say maybe twenty minutes. Thirty at the most. It doesn't matter though because I'm no closer to figuring a way out than I was the moment he locked the door behind him.

As I stare at the ceiling, straining to hear anything beyond the thundering of my heartbeat and throbbing of my head, I force myself to remember who I was with when I was taken, who was on their way to us as we rode to the clubhouse.

The Soulless Kings MC. They knew where we were, Royal made sure of it when he shared his location. But is it still transmitting? Are they close?

"Ahhhh," I cry out, when out of nowhere, a piercing

pain stabs through my heart, obliterating me into millions of fragments.

We'd know.

No!

The door flies open, and Brock casually walks in without closing it behind him.

"Do that again," he demands.

I struggle against the chains, sobs erupting from deep in my belly, carrying my soul as they leave my body.

"No, not that," he tsks. "Scream. I like it when you scream."

"Y-you're as c-crazy as Al-Alice," I stammer, my throat clogging.

"And now you're going to be as alone as I am."

"He w-was alive. R-Royal was alive."

"You got me." Brock shrugs as he sits on the edge of the cot. "He was alive. But now he's not."

We'd know.

I know!

"Kill me," I beg, unbearable anguish weighing me down like a ton of bricks.

"I will," he says. "In time, I will kill you."

"He didn't d-deserve to die," I wail. "He's t-too good. Good p-p-people do b-bad things."

Brock lifts the blanket from the floor where he left it earlier and covers me. Where he was vile before, he's oddly half-decent now. He brushes the hair out of my face and shushes me as I cry.

He and Alice were the perfect pair.

"I'm gonna give you a few minutes to grieve your loss." His tone suggests he's doing me a favor. But I don't want his favor. I don't want anything from him except death. "And then I'm going to torture you for a while before I kill you."

Royal

"Or you can just go straight to Hell."

My breath hitches, and I whip my head toward the door. Flash and Greaser are standing there, both with guns trained on Brock.

"You okay, Paige?" Greaser asks, his attention solely focused on the man sitting next to me.

"He k-killed Royal."

"No, darlin', he didn't," Flash says.

"I did," Brock says, seemingly unconcerned that there are two guns aimed at his skull.

A gunshot echoes off the walls, and it takes me a second to register that Brock is now slumped on the floor, as dead as Royal.

Both Flash and Greaser rush forward. Greaser drags Brock toward the wall while Flash works to unlock the chains.

"Sorry about that," he says in a calm tone. "He was pissing me off."

"Hurry it up. We need to get that fucker back to the clubhouse so Gibson has more space to work if there's any hope of him surviving this."

Flash looks over his shoulder, and I follow his gaze. Fender is standing there, blood soaking through his shirt and jeans. "Gimme another thirty seconds."

Fender nods and dashes out of sight.

"Hope of who surviving?" I ask as the last chain lock clicks open.

"Royal," Greaser says as he lifts me into his arms. "We got here just in time. He's in bad shape, but Gibson's a damn good doctor. Royal is gonna be just fine, but we've gotta go."

"But he's—"

"Not dead," Flash snaps. "He's not fucking dead."

"Dude, get it together," Greaser barks. "She's not thinking clearly."

He's right. I'm not. Royal died. I felt it. I *knew* it the moment it happened.

But they're telling you he's alive. So maybe...

Greaser sets me in the back of the van, and chaos surrounds me. Gibson is frantically working to keep Royal alive. Fender is barking orders into his phone, Piston is driving, and Flash and Greaser are staring at me as if I've sprouted two heads.

The ride to the clubhouse is bumpy, agonizing, but I don't care. All I care about is Royal.

"When we get back, Gibson's wife, Alena, is going to check you out, okay?"

I nod absently at Fender.

"She's worked alongside him for a while now. She might not be able to do anything major, but at least she can get any cuts and scrapes cleaned up. And when Gibson is done working on Royal, he'll give you a more thorough exam."

Again, I nod.

"Paige, I need you to tell me you hear me," Fender says.

"I he-hear you."

"Good."

Greaser carries me into the clubhouse when we arrive, and Flash and Piston carry Royal. We're separated, and I don't like it, but I'm too weak to argue.

I sit for two hours, numb, as Alena disinfects the road rash from the crash, and tends to any other superficial wounds she finds. I whimper from the pain, but otherwise, I'm silent.

"Paige, I think you're going to need stitches on your cheek," Alena says, her quiet tone soothing. "But I'd rather Gibson do that, if that's okay."

"When can I see him?"

"Gibson?"

"Royal," I clarify. "When can I see him?"

"I'll take you to him now, if that's what you want."

"Yes, please."

"Let's get you dressed first."

Alena helps me into a pair of sweats that are too long, and a hoodie that could fit two of me in. She leads me down the hall to another room on the second floor. Gibson is sitting in a chair next to the bed, and Fender is leaning against the wall with his arms crossed over his chest.

Royal is lying in bed, a sheet pulled up to mid-chest. He's got an IV coming out of his hand, and he's hooked up to beeping machines. The sound would be incredibly annoying if it weren't the only sign that Royal is, indeed, alive.

"Hey, Paige," Fender greets when he sees me. "I know it looks bad, but he's going to be okay."

Gibson rises from his chair and walks toward me. "I'm keeping him sedated for now, just to get him through the worst of it. Hopefully I can reduce the sedation in a few days."

"Okay."

"You can talk to him if you want." Gibson shrugs. "I don't know if he can hear you or not, but I figure it can't hurt, just in case."

"Okay."

"We'll give you some time."

Fender and Gibson leave, and I sit in the chair Gibson vacated. I lift Royal's hand in mine and am surprised by how cold it is. The bruising and lacerations on his throat send a shiver of stark fear from my head to my toes.

"I need you to breathe for me, Royal," I whisper brokenly. "I need you to keep breathing."

Tears stream down my cheeks. I don't know how long I sit there, holding his hand, but I'm startled and jump back when a throat is cleared behind me.

"Sorry, I didn't mean to scare you," Flash says as he steps up next to me. "How's he doing?"

"Gibson said he'll be okay."

"Good."

I look up at Flash. "Thank you. I don't know if I said that yet but thank you for saving me too."

"It's what we do, Paige. You're Royal's, so you're ours too. Family, Paige. Soulless Kings will always come for family."

"Well, thanks." I wrinkle my nose. "How did you find us?"

Flash frowns. "I can't really tell you. Club business and all that."

"Oh."

"Let's just say we have connections, and with some *encouragement*, those connections came through."

"I don't know what that means."

"And that's how it's supposed to be."

"Okay."

There are a lot of things I don't know or understand about the club and how they work. But I'm learning. And I want to keep learning.

"Ya know, Royal played the hero in my story," Flash says quietly. "I don't know if he told you that, but he did. I'm glad I got to be one in his story. He can be a pain in the ass sometimes, but he's a good guy. It'd been a hell of a thing to lose him."

"Yeah." I glance at a sedated Royal. "A hell of a thing."

Royal

"Try to get some rest, Paige," Flash encourages. "Stay with him if you want but try to rest. You need to heal too."

Flash leaves, and I stay right where I am. I don't know if I'll be able to rest or not, but as long as Royal is in this bed, I'm going to be in this room.

"Royal," I whisper, leaning down close to his ear. "I need you to be okay."

I press a kiss to his cheek and rest my forehead on the spot my lips touched.

"I need you to be okay because I think I'm in love with you."

Chapter Twenty Five

Torture. Sweet, exquisite, sinful torture.

Royal

Two months later...

"All clear."

I grin at Gibson. He's been providing all my medical care since everything went down with Brock. I will have permanent scars on my neck from the rope, but over time, they'll fade. And Paige calls my stab wounds sexy battle scars, so I don't stress about those. Maybe I'll get tattoos to cover them, but for now, they're the least of my worries.

My woman, on the other hand, and tonight? That's a worry.

Or a hope.

"You're sure?" I ask, not wanting my hopes to soar too high.

"Yeah, brother." He slaps me on the back. "I'm sure. Go home, get laid. You've earned it."

Royal

"You have no idea," I groan, hopping off the exam table he now keeps at the clubhouse.

Paige and I have been taking things slow since the event. That's what we call it, the event. If it had been up to me, I'd have moved in with her immediately. We'd been practically living together before I was almost murdered, but Paige insisted that she needed to be on her own.

I didn't understand at first. She'd lived alone for years. But she explained that she'd spent so much of her time and energy on Alice, and she was afraid to move too fast and get enmeshed with someone else. She made it clear that she loved me, but she needed time.

So I gave her time. I gave her two months to be exact. But that ends tonight. Because a week ago, Paige informed me that as soon as Gibson gives me the all clear, she's ready. Honestly, I think she was physically ready long before then, but I wasn't going to push. She's too important.

"Yo, Royal?"

I stop with my hand on the door, one bike ride between me and the love of my life, and turn to face Parker.

"What's up?"

"I know you're heading out, but Sully and Bruno are on their way over," he says, referring to the two most recent prospects. We spent a lot more time with them before issuing an official invite, not wanting a repeat of Benny, and they've been great. "I know you've got shit planned for them in a few days, but anything I can help with while you're, um... otherwise occupied?"

"Don't care, prospect," I tell him. "Trainwreck is covering for me tonight and tomorrow. Ask him."

At church this morning, and in anticipation of me getting Gibson's medical all clear, Fender ordered everyone to leave me alone for the next forty-eight hours because he doesn't want to stand between a cock and pussy. His words, not mine. And if anyone repeats them to Paige, I'll cut out their heart.

The ride to the loft seems to take forever, and after I park next to her car in the parking garage, I practically skip across the street to get to her. I bypass the elevator and take the steps two at a time, and when I reach the door to the loft, I stop to take a deep breath.

Should I knock? Use my key? What the hell do I do now?

My nerves jangle, and I rub my sweaty palms on my jeans. The only time I ever use my key is if I come over and she's not home from work yet. But I don't ever knock either when she's home. I did the first few times, but then she started getting annoyed because I'd usually be interrupting her while she was in her dark room. I don't like to annoy her, so I stopped.

Before I make up my mind, the door slides open, and I swallow my tongue.

Paige is standing there in only a pair of black bikini panties. Yes, just panties.

I'm a lucky fucking man.

She grabs my shirt and yanks me inside. "Gibson texted me and said you were good," she says, and the sultriness in her voice is on point. "Please tell me he wasn't messing with me," she pleads.

I shake my head.

"Thank God."

Paige jumps up and wraps her legs around my waist, giving me no choice but to catch her, and I fuse my lips to hers as I carry her to the bedroom. She darts her tongue into my mouth, and I suck it deeper, swirling mine around it.

When my shins hit the bed, I pull my mouth free and

drop her onto the mattress. I make quick work of stripping out of my clothes, and when my cock is free, her eyes widen.

"Aw, sugar, you're gonna love it," I croon as I lean over her, urging her onto her back. "I promise."

Paige moans as I drag my dick up the inside of her thigh, and when I'm met with cloth, I yank them so hard, they rip from her body.

"Oh my."

Oh my, indeed.

"I know I should take this slow," I say. "Fuck, I know it. But I don't know if I can, Paige."

She cups my cheeks and pulls me close. "I don't want slow, Royal. I don't want it at all. Not tonight. I just want you... inside of me... now. We've waited long enough."

I reach between our bodies and line my cock up with her entrance. I know what she said, but my mind screams at me to not listen. It screams at me to make this special, but Paige doesn't seem to give a damn about what my mind is screaming because she grabs my hips and pulls me forward and she thrusts her hips up.

"We've waited long enough," she repeats breathlessly.

Torture. Sweet, exquisite, sinful torture. Paige's pussy is slick, and snug, and perfectly made for me.

Despite how hard she tries to speed things up, and my concerns about my inability to last long enough, I force my movements to remain slow, controlled. Gliding in and out of her, I brace my hands on either side of her head. Her lips part, and her eyes slide closed.

It's on the tip of my tongue to command her to look at me, but I know that's a triggering phrase, so I refrain. This is our time, not our memories' time.

I rock my hips to ensure her clit is part of the action, and she digs her nails into my ass. And when I bury myself balls deep, she holds me steady while she rolls her hips in a circle.

"Make me come, Royal," she pleads. "Please make me come."

Slow flies out the window in response to her request, and I pull out until the only thing remaining is my tip, and then I thrust, hard. I set a punishing pace, but Paige keeps up, her hips matching the rhythm of mine.

Reaching between us again, I press my thumb to her clit, rubbing fast circles over the sensitive nub. Paige throws her head back, and her neck strains. I lean forward and lick the pulsing vein, the throbbing in her throat mimicking the throbbing of my dick.

I focus on every single movement I make, every single telltale flutter of her walls, and when the slightest change occurs, I increase my efforts. I fuck her hard, fast, and deep. I overwhelm her senses, and my own.

When her pussy clenches and her legs shake, I let myself go, unable to hold back while she's coming. Paige groans incoherently, and I roar as I spill inside of her.

Holy. Shit.

Each of us uses the other to ride out the aftershocks, each taking what we need, each giving equally. My vision tunnels for a minute, but it widens as I collapse on top of her, utterly spent.

Paige tries to move, but I'm too heavy, so I roll to the side, tucking her against my chest as I do.

"You've got five minutes to recover," she says drowsily. "And then we're doing that again."

I chuckle. "I can handle that."

"Royal?"

"Yeah, sugar?"

"That was worth the wait."

Epilogue

They say your life flashes before your eyes at the moment just before death. They fucking lied.

Royal
Fifteen years later...

"Where the hell does the time go?"

I wrap my arms around Paige's waist and hug her to me. Her back rests against my chest, and she sighs.

"I don't know, sugar. Time flies when you're having fun."

Paige and I have been married for thirteen years, and our daughter, Linnie, turned ten last month. We had a party to celebrate, and it was every bit as hectic as the party we're at now. Birthdays are a big deal for the Soulless Kings, and it seems we have one almost every week.

"Remember the day he was born?" Paige asks me.

"You mean the day Fender swore he was getting a

vasectomy because he couldn't handle watching Charlie in so much pain?"

She laughs. "Yeah. Jax was so tiny and look at him now. Turning fifteen and wishing his life away."

"Paige, every fifteen-year-old boy wants to be older. Charlie and Harley were the same when they turned fifteen, but they wisened up a little."

Trainwreck and Sylvia's twin boys aren't all that wise, but give 'em a few more years, and they'll make damn fine Soulless Kings. I have to admit, watching Trainwreck navigate fatherhood reminded me of all the stupid shit he used to do as a prospect, all the ways he earned his road name. So if he can grow into the man he is today, so can his boys.

But it is a trainwreck for sure.

"Hey, Royal!"

I turn to see Trenton, Greaser and Trinity's son walking toward us.

"T, when'd you get here? Your dad said you had finals to finish before you could make the drive."

"Yeah, well, I lied to him," he says with a laugh. "I wanted to surprise Jax, and I knew if I told either of my parents, they'd blab."

"Do they know you're here?" Paige asks.

"Yeah. I talked to them for a few minutes. I'll get to visit more later. Right now I just want to see everyone and celebrate Jax's birthday."

He disappears into the crowd, and I watch him go. All the Soulless Kings' children are growing up way too fast. The oldest is thirty, and the youngest, six. Paige asked me where the time has gone, and I just don't know.

But I wish I could get some of it back. Time is precious, and not to be wasted.

As I watch Tori, Joker and Riley's six-year-old daughter

laugh as Ali, Flash and Jaci's twenty-two-year-old daughter, pushes her on the swings, I think back to the days when Linnie was a newborn.

Paige and I had been living in the loft for six years when she learned she was pregnant. We'd talked about moving, but never took the plunge. Needing a nursery was the push we needed. We still live in a loft, only this one is much bigger, and we still own her old loft and the building it's in. Only it now boasts a business sign that reads 'Royally Watkins Studio', and the rest of the building is used as a gallery for young and upcoming photographers who need a little leg up getting started in their careers.

Linnie was a small baby, and at ten, she's still small for her age. But like her mama, she's mighty. And she's loyal and brave and too kind for her own good sometimes.

But I wouldn't change her for anything.

Despite the numerous sleepless nights, worried tears, and almost heart attacks.

"Do you still have church later?" Paige asks.

"Yeah. I think Fender's starting to feel his age. He's not ready to throw in the towel, but he knows we need to start preparing the next generation to take over."

"I can't believe the next generation is even old enough, or close to old enough, *to* take over."

"Neither can I."

Piston and Holland are the only other couple with children. Des and Devin, the brothers they took in years ago, are thirty and twenty-four. Ali has had a crush on Devin since she was old enough to talk, but I don't think anything will come of that. Not if Flash has anything to say about it. Christopher and Zula are in their late teens and early twenties, respectively, and very close with Des and Devin.

They're all grown. All of them. It boggles my mind.

Every time I walk past the photographs hanging in the clubhouse, I'm transported back in time to the moment it reflects, the moment Paige managed to capture and freeze. And with each memory, I'm reminded of how grateful I am to have this family, to be a Soulless King.

Aside from Paige, changing the course of my life and prospecting for an MC, *this* MC, was the best decision I ever made.

They say your life flashes before your eyes at the moment just before death. The fucking lied.

They did get one thing right though, whoever *they* are. Life *is* a series of flashes, millions upon millions of split-second snapshots that make up what we call memories. Some people, like my ol' lady, capture those moments in photographs that we can all look at and enjoy, while others rely on all the parts of their brain required to hold onto the moments and never let go.

And then there are people like me, like my brothers. We choose to live out in the wide open, to experience the split-seconds as they happen because we can't look backward, and we can't look forward. Yesterday is over, and tomorrow is never guaranteed. If we've learned anything as bikers, it's that.

Life flashes before your eyes every single second of every single day.

So, I'll say it again for those of you in the back...

They say your life flashes before your eyes at the moment just before death.

They. Fucking. Lied.

Next in the Soulless Kings MC

Oh, snap... Royal is the final book.

Or is it?

You guessed it! More Soulless Kings MC will be coming your way soon.

I don't know about you, but I love this world, this biker family. Ending it completely just wasn't sitting right with me, so I figure, why end it? Why not just shift things around a bit and give the world some fresh blood? And that's exactly what I intend to do!

While we are saying goodbye to our favorite men in the Oregon Chapter, we'll be saying a big fat HELLO to the brothers in the Marble Falls, Texas Chapter. You met them in Flash (book #9), and it won't be long before they're gracing a Kindle or bookshelf near you.

Beginning in early 2024, Soulless Kings MC: Marble Falls, TX will kick off with their president, Crow. Stay tuned to my social media and/or website for all updates!

If you loved Soulless Kings MC, check out Satan's Legacy MC:

Snow's Angel: Book #1

Snow...

As the president of Satan's Legacy MC, I have an image to maintain, responsibilities that pull me over to the wrong side of the law. We're one percenters and damn proud of it. But I have a weakness for women and children in need. I found a way to turn that weakness into a positive for the club and our community, but what the hell am I supposed to do this Christmas season when it threatens to bring me to my knees?

Sami...

Be a good mother. That's all I've ever wanted. I haven't always made the best decisions. The worst one cost me seven years and my independence, but that's over now. But

If you loved Soulless Kings MC, check out Satan's Legacy MC:

how am I supposed to be a good mother when my son and I are left to pick up the pieces on the streets of Denver with no money, no roof over our heads, no food, no nothing? An unlikely knight in leather armor comes to our rescue, but can I trust him? He's balls deep in some scary shit, and I don't know if I can withstand the storm that follows him.

Snow's Angel: Chapter 1
Sami

"You can't be serious?"

Fear settles in my gut like a lead weight. It's two in the morning and Lennox is sound asleep, thank God. Corey is pacing, rage rolling off of him in waves.

"I want you both out," Corey shouts, loud enough to wake our son up.

"It's the middle of the night," I argue. "Where are we supposed to go?"

Corey advances on me and wraps his fingers around my throat and squeezes. "I don't give a fuck where you and the brat go. Go fucking die for all I care."

I claw at his hand and struggle to suck air into my lungs. This isn't the first rage of Corey's that I've been on the receiving end of. Hell, this isn't even the first time he's kicked us out. It is, however, the first time he's done it in the middle of the night.

A creaking noise reaches my ears and I let my eyes slide closed because I know what that means. Corey's black eyes shift from me to our son, who's standing in the hallway. He releases me but not without quickly squeezing against my windpipe one last time. I stumble back a few steps and take several deep breaths before turning to face Lennox.

"You're supposed to be in bed, baby," I scold, trying to sound like our world isn't crumbling.

"What are you guys fighting about this time?" Lennox asks.

I cringe at the way he makes it sound so normal. Like the fact that he just witnessed his father try to choke me out is an everyday occurrence.

"Nothing." I silently pray that he doesn't ask more questions or that Corey says anything about—

"You and your mom are leaving." So much for answered prayers. Corey stomps out of the room but makes sure to dig the knife in deeper. "You've got five minutes to get your shit and go."

The back door slamming rattles the walls, and I flinch at the finality of it. I rush to Lennox's side and try to wrap my arms around him, but he shrinks away from me.

"What did you do?" he asks with all the attitude of a seven-year-old boy with Corey Devlin's blood running through his veins.

"Nothing," I snap. "Hurry up and go put your shoes on."

I urge him toward his bedroom, but he digs in his heels. "I don't wanna leave."

I heave a sigh and swallow past the lump in my throat. Of course he'd want to stay with his dad. Corey is the fun parent. Sure, he's also an awful parent, but for some reason, that's not how Lennox sees him. Much to my dismay, Lennox idolizes his dad, and I'm terrified that he's going to end up just like him.

"I don't care what you want, Lennox." I use my harshest

mom voice because right now, we need to go. There's no time for this argument. "Get your shoes."

"Fine," he huffs and stomps to his room.

I look toward the back door and see Corey pacing on the patio. I can see him holding the cordless phone to his ear, smiling as he talks. Two minutes ago he was ready to kill me and now he looks like he's happy as can be. I shake away the thought. It doesn't matter. He's dangerous and I'd do well to remember that.

I rush around the house to grab up anything I can, anything that will fit in the small duffel bag I have. It's the same bag I left home with at sixteen, the one I shoved in the back seat of Corey's rusted out Chevy. I was pregnant and full of rebellion because my parents wanted me to abort our baby. I don't regret my decision to have my son. But I do regret thinking I needed to be with his dad because of it.

"I'm ready."

I whirl around and see a sullen Lennox standing behind me, tattered second-hand Nike's on his feet and a ratty old teddy bear that he's had since he was born. I try to reconcile the little boy holding a stuffed animal with the boy that is so much like his dad. I remind myself that somewhere in Lennox is my DNA, and without Corey's influence, maybe he'll change. God help me if he doesn't.

I lift the royal blue winter coat off the couch and thrust it at him. "Here, put this on."

"I don't need no jacket."

"It's December in Colorado and it's cold out."

"I'm not wearing a damn jacket." Lennox crosses his arms over his chest, his teddy bear squished against his tiny body.

I drop my head and take a few deep breaths to steady myself. *He's acting out, Sami. Once we're away from Corey, he'll be better.* I repeat that in my head, over and over again, until I convince myself that I believe it.

"Put the coat on. Now."

Apparently, the harshness in my tone is enough to make him second-guess if this is an argument he wants to continue. He yanks the jacket out of my hands and does as he's told. While he's doing that, I search the room for my own coat and come up empty. Damn, where did I leave it?

I jump at the unmistakable sound of the back door creaking open. Forgetting my own warning to Lennox about the cold, I sling the duffel bag over my shoulder and grab my son's hand to drag him out the front door into the frigid Colorado winter temperatures.

Neither of us say a word as we trudge down the street, past the rundown houses of our neighbors. I don't let myself look back until we reach the corner. Just before we turn right, I glance behind me. My shoulders sag when I see that our front yard is empty. Silly me thought that maybe, just maybe, Corey would regret kicking us out and coming running after us.

It's better this way, Sami. You're free. You and Lennox are freezing, but you're free.

"Where are we going?"

Lennox's teeth chatter as he speaks. I don't allow myself to stop walking and answer him until we've gotten down another block. When I do stop, I crouch down and look into my son's blue eyes. I've never lied to my son, and I don't intend to start now.

"I don't know."

I rub my hands up and down his arms, trying like hell to warm him up as best I can. I ignore the tingling in my own body. I've been out in the cold before, although I was the kid in that situation and not the parent.

Snow's Angel: Chapter 1

"I don't know why I had to come," Lennox whines. "Dad woulda let me stay."

I clench my jaw, forcing the words that are on the tip of my tongue to stay where they are. I grew up with parents who hated each other, and I promised myself I wouldn't act like them with my own son. An idea hits me, and I smile as widely as my shivering will allow.

"Why don't we treat this like an adventure?"

"Mom." Lennox drags the word out dramatically.

As my plan solidifies in my brain, I reach for my purse, which is usually slung over my shoulder when I'm not at home and am met with nothing.

"Dammit!"

"What?" Lennox narrows his eyes.

"Nothing, baby."

I think back over everything that happened when I got home from work at the diner. I walked inside and Corey had immediately started yelling at me. I remember being tired and wanting to do nothing but get off of my feet after a long day but that wasn't going to happen once he got into his tirade. It was the same old shit. I'm never home, he's always gotta take care of 'the brat', he needed money for a fix and—

Shit! He yanked my purse off of my shoulder to rifle through it for money. And I bet it's on the floor, right where he tossed it after he stole my thirty-six dollars in tips.

I glance at my son and paste a smile on my face. It's going to be okay. Everything is going to be just fine. We have no money, no place to go, and it's frigid outside. But we're good.

I tip my head back and stare at the sky, silently praying for whoever or whatever is up there to throw me a bone, give me a sign as to what I'm supposed to do to fix this.

Snow's Angel: Chapter 1

After a few seconds, something wet hits my cheek and I know that was the higher power's way of flipping me the bird.

Big, fat snowflakes cascade out of the black expanse above us. I grab Lennox's hand and pull him along with me as I continue to walk farther from our home.

After trudging through the cold for a few miles, we're closer to downtown, and while the thought of the city in the middle of the night is scary, it's our only option. Maybe we'll get lucky and the shelter on Third street will let us in.

The longer we walk, the slower our steps become. I finally see the sign for the shelter ahead, and relief washes over me. My fingers and toes are numb, my legs burn, and my vision is starting to blur. I want to stop, to lie down right where I am, but the small hand in mine is what keeps me going.

When we reach the door, I try to lift my arm to knock, as the sign posted on the wood instructs, but it's impossible.

"B-b-baby, go a-ahead."

I struggle to form words as my teeth chatter but am grateful when my son's hand leaves mine. Before his fist connects with the wooden barrier that separates us from warmth, I give in to the unrelenting cold. I feel myself fall. I feel the wet snow seep through the fabric of my clothes. I feel everything as if it's happening in slow motion and I'm powerless to stop it.

At least I can die knowing I got my baby to safety.

About the Author

Andi Rhodes is an author whose passion is creating romance from chaos in all her books! She writes MC (motorcycle club) romance with a generous helping of suspense and doesn't shy away from the more difficult topics. Her books can be triggering for some so consider yourself warned. Andi also ensures each book ends with the couple getting their HEA! Most importantly, Andi is living her real life HEA with her husband and their boxers.

For access to release info and updates, be sure to Andi's website at www.andirhodes.com.

Also by Andi Rhodes

Broken Rebel Brotherhood

Broken Souls

Broken Innocence

Broken Boundaries

Broken Rebel Brotherhood: Complete Series Box set

Broken Rebel Brotherhood: Next Generation

Broken Hearts

Broken Wings

Broken Mind

Bastards and Badges

Stark Revenge

Slade's Fall

Jett's Guard

Soulless Kings MC

Fender

Joker

Piston

Greaser

Riker

Trainwreck

Squirrel

Gibson

Flash

Royal

Satan's Legacy MC

Snow's Angel

Toga's Demons

Magic's Torment

Duck's Salvation

Dip's Flame

Devil's Handmaidens MC

Harlow's Gamble

Peppermint's Twist

Mama's Rules

Valhalla Rising MC

Viking

Mayhem Makers

Forever Savage

Saints Purgatory MC

Unholy Soul

Printed in Great Britain
by Amazon

44178518R00128